CW01083097

NAKED IN

HIGH HEELS

A NUDIST NOVELLA BY

CRESSIDA TWITCHETT

========================

FOR
SALLY

CHAPTER ONE

Being naked in public was not Cassie Pulaski's idea of a good time. It was not as if she had a body to be ashamed of. At twenty-four, she was slender and smooth and firm although hardly voluptuous. Luckily for her, it was the Sixties and being young and slim was very fashionable. In fact, with her small breasts, narrow hips, elfin haircut and dark brown eyes, Cassie had often been compared to the iconic model Twiggy back home in London. She loved living in London in the swinging Sixties even though she existed only on the very fringe of the swinging scene. But now she was in a somewhat different environment where swinging was confined to various body parts. Cassie was somewhere in France in the middle of a nudist colony and she was about to take her first steps out into a world of nakedness.

Cassie had not become a nudist by choice. She was on an assignment. She was a spy, although to call her a secret agent was something of an exaggeration. She normally worked in a fairly boring clerical position deep within the bowels of British Counter Intelligence, an organisation comprised almost entirely of eccentrics and misfits. Cassie only had a job there as a favour to her mother who had been a very effective operative during the war. It was on one of her operations that Mum had become involved with an American agent and upset her superiors by taking maternity leave at a fairly busy time. While Mum waited for Cassie to be born, Daddy parachuted behind enemy lines and was never seen again. Because unmarried mothers were frowned on in those days, Mum took his name and bought herself a wedding ring. Baby Cassie was handed over to her bohemian Aunt Connie to be raised while Mum resumed her illustrious career.

Mum continued to be a spy all through the Cold War until, when Cassie was nineteen, she also failed to return from a mission. Cassie became an orphan whose employment prospects did not seem to extend beyond working behind the cosmetics counter at Woolworths. So the secret service, in a rare display of guilty responsibility, offered Cassie a job. It involved typing and filing and occasionally searching for patterns in material collected by agents in the field. She was not overly proficient in any of these tasks but her bubbly personality and the organisation's debt to her mother seemed to guarantee that she had a job until the day she either found another one or got married. Neither of those alternatives seemed likely in the short term. Cassie was too busy enjoying herself, which was the primary objective for someone of her age in 1967.

Her carefree existence was rudely interrupted by a summons to the office of the head of Counter Intelligence, a tall thin military type with untamed hair and large horn-rimmed glasses on his skull-like face. The staff had various nicknames for him, none of which were flattering, but in his presence he was simply Sir Alistair. Cassie had never before spoken to him let alone been to his inner sanctum. She entered his office like a bashful ghost and was slightly unnerved to see not just the master but two other equally imposing figures, one of whom she recognised as secret agent John Fraser who she had developed a crush on merely by reading his file.

Sir Alistair motioned for Cassie to sit in an uncomfortable chair in the middle of the room after which the three men surrounded her and towered over her like a trio of vultures trying to decide if her little body was worth the effort. Cassie felt a sudden urge to pee but knew that asking to be excused was not an option. She tried to make eye contact with the grey-suited trinity but could not manage it. Instead, she looked down at her trendy white shoes with the kitten heels and waited for what seemed like an eternity for someone to speak.

"How long have you been with us, Miss Pulaski?" Sir Alistair finally asked in an almost friendly tone.

"Almost three years," Cassie replied with a very dry throat.

"Do you like working here?"

Unable to find her voice, Cassie nodded slightly then thought it a good idea to nod again with more enthusiasm.

"Our work is very important," Sir Alistair intoned as though he was beginning a speech. "We keep the country safe."

There was not much Cassie could say in reply to that.

"Do you love your country?" The question sounded almost like an accusation.

"Yes, of course," Cassie mumbled. "I think it's fab."

"You're half American," the unknown man with the shiny bald head said.

"I know my father was an American," Cassie struggled to say, "but that's really all I know about him. I've never even been to America. I've always thought of myself as being British and nothing else."

"Good answer," said John Fraser with a slight smile that helped Cassie to relax just a little bit. "I think we've found our girl."

"Yes," Sir Alistair nodded gravely. "She's the right age, the right sort all right - very typical of her type but not very tall."

"I'm five foot three," Cassie interjected, drawing glances of admonishment from the men, "but I can wear heels."

"But she has no experience," the bald man said.

"That's what makes her so right," Fraser replied sharply. "All of our field agents would run the risk of being recognised. We need someone who is a complete unknown to the opposition and especially to the Fox."

Cassie remembered seeing the name of the Fox in various files. From what she could recall, the Fox had long been a thorn in the side of Counter Intelligence.

"Miss Pulaski," Sir Alistair was now addressing her with unusual politeness, "your mother was one of our finest agents. We are hoping that some of her talent and resourcefulness and, yes, courage, has rubbed off on you. Do you think that's possible?"

Once again, Cassie was left speechless. The desire to pee intensified as she waited to hear what was coming next.

"We want you to go undercover for us in a manner of speaking," Sir Alistair continued as he sat on the edge of his desk. "We wouldn't ask this of you if it were not vitally important. For the first time in a long time, we have the chance to stop, and hopefully eliminate, one of the West's most dangerous enemies. We are hoping that you can help us in this endeavour."

"What can I do?" Cassie asked nervously.

"This person we call the Fox has been traced to a location in France," Fraser explained in a calm voice.

"Your mother did some of her best work in France," Sir Alistair added.

"No one knows who the Fox is or what he looks like," Fraser continued. "We're not absolutely sure if the Fox is male or female. But we're reasonably certain that he or she is lying low in this location in preparation for something big. Our only hope of stopping it is by identifying the Fox."

"That's where you come in," said Sir Alistair. "This location is relatively small, little more than a village, but it's a holiday location. People from various countries come and go all the time. When you think about it, it's actually quite a clever hiding place and, as such, it's a place that can only be infiltrated by someone the Fox would have no reason to suspect."

"A young English girl on holiday," the bald man said with a strange smirk-like smile as he looked Cassie up and down.

"It sounds dangerous," Cassie stammered.

"It will not be necessary for you to confront the Fox," Sir Alistair replied reassuringly, "only to expose him."

"And how do I do that?" asked a worried Cassie.

"By being very clever," smiled Sir Alistair. "You're a very personable young lady – mix with everyone and look for clues that someone is not quite right. Use your instincts and your intuition. Your mother always had such wonderful instincts and intuitions."

"I'm not my mother," Cassie said defensively.

"You're the child of two very talented secret agents," Sir Alistair replied. "I feel confident that once you are on the ground, you will know just what to do."

"I'll be nearby if you need me," Fraser added.

"Not too nearby," Baldy said. "We mustn't do anything that might alert the Fox to what's going on."

Suddenly, there was a long silence. Cassie found it impossible to look directly at any of the three men, not even the marginally handsome John Fraser. Instead, she stared out the window whose view was mostly blocked by a flowering chestnut tree. Her heart was pounding inside her tiny breast and hands were moist. She was dying for a cigarette but did not dare ask for one. Instead, she nervously uncrossed and re-crossed her legs, only then realising just how short her miniskirt was.

"Will you do it?" Sir Alistair finally asked.

Cassie felt a sudden and unusual surge of patriotism and love for the Queen and the Union Jack. "I suppose it will be kind of like getting a free holiday," she shrugged.

"Good girl," said Sir Alistair as though addressing a household pet. "Fraser will brief you on all the details and give you a bit of training. You leave the day after tomorrow."

Sir Alistair extended his hand towards her and Cassie shook it limply as she rose to her not very steady feet. Fraser took her by the arm and led her from the room. Once she was gone, Sir Alistair sat behind his desk and lit a large meerschaum pipe whose foul odour quickly filled the office.

"Do you think it will work?" the bald man asked.

"I'd say the odds are fifty-fifty," Sir Alistair replied thoughtfully. "At worst, she will provide a distraction for our actual operation."

"She could get killed," said the bald man as he prepared to leave.

"In that case," Sir Alistair said in between puffs, "we will lose one of our least efficient employees – something that should please you bean counters at the ministry."

Once Cassie left the office, her primary concern was finding a toilet. As it happened, the only available one was an unoccupied men's room where she found it prudent to hold her breath. As soon as that need was satisfied, she joined Fraser is a small and otherwise deserted waiting room with painfully out of date furniture. Her first thought was to ask him for a cigarette and he offered her an American brand from a posh silver cigarette case. Cassie inhaled and exhaled slowly a couple of times, completely savouring the nicotine effect, then managed a little smile of relief as she glanced towards her new colleague.

John Fraser was not classically handsome but he was far from repulsive. As a secret agent, he tried hard not to appear distinctive in any way but his attempts to be ordinary were not completely successful. He possessed a very masculine aura that went beyond mere looks. He was slightly less than six feet tall and very physically fit. His dark blonde hair was an inch or two longer than most men but much shorter than most of the boys that Cassie knew. Fraser seemed very straight and business-like but his smile, which was frequent, had a suggestion of mischief in its crooked lines. His blue eyes revealed a wealth of worldly experience. He had a deep, gravelly voice and had obviously worked hard at removing all traces of a regional accent. He was a good spy because he was good at deceit. Cassie idly wondered how many women he had slept with and how many of them were because of duty and whether he was capable of love.

"The old man didn't say so," Fraser said to her, "but we're very grateful for what you're doing."

"I have no idea what I'm doing," Cassie replied as the reality of her situation finally dawned on her.

"You'll be fine," Fraser smiled. "You just have to remember to keep your eyes and ears open at all times. With luck, it will all be over in a few days."

"Where exactly am I going?"

"A little place down in Languedoc called Le Soleil d'Or," Fraser replied like a travel agent.

"The Golden Sun," Cassie whispered to herself.

"That's right."

"I've been to France many times," Cassie said, "but I can't say I've ever heard of it."

"It's a bit off the beaten path," Fraser replied, "which is probably why the Fox chose it."

"How do I get there?" Cassie asked with a worried frown. "I don't have to parachute or anything, do I?"

"Don't worry," laughed Fraser. "It's friendly territory. We'll give you a car. You cross the channel on a ferry and drive there. I'll give you directions."

"One little problem," Cassie said in a quiet voice. "I don't have a driving license."

"Seriously?" replied Fraser. "How do you get about?"

"Public transport," shrugged Cassie.

"We'll work something out," said Fraser with reassuring confidence. "The important thing is that once you're there, you blend in. I assume you're not overly modest."

"What do you mean?" Cassie asked, slightly puzzled.

Fraser drew in a deep breath and looked her straight in the eyes. "Le Soleil d'Or is a nudist colony."

Cassie gasped loudly then tried to reply but found that she had no voice. She had never been averse to wearing a bikini on holiday and had even gone topless on occasion. Whatever carefree American genes she might have inherited were balanced by her natural British sense of embarrassment that made her reluctant to show off her naked body except when madly in love or under the influence of too many gin and tonics.

"You are joking," she finally managed to stammer.

"Sorry," Fraser shrugged. "That's why this seems like such a perfect opportunity to, shall we say, expose the Fox. He's always been a master of disguise."

"That's a good trick in a nudist colony," Cassie said, still trying to catch her breath and absent-mindedly pulling on the hem of her miniskirt.

"Exactly."

There was another long pause in their conversation. Suddenly the prospect of encountering a dangerous enemy agent seemed less intimidating than being stark naked in the midst of a lot of other naked people. The worst part was that she would be alone. She might not mind so much if Fraser was there with her. She could easily be persuaded to be naked with him and would quite like to know what was underneath that Savile Row suit. But being alone in a nudist colony seemed too much like the makings of a nightmare.

"Couldn't I take one of my friends with me, you know, another girl?" she half said and half mumbled.

"Sorry," shrugged Fraser, debating with himself about the wisdom of putting an arm around her. "You're not going to change your mind, are you?"

"And risk Old Misery Guts sending me to the Tower for treason?" said Cassie with an attempted smile. "No fear. Although I'm surprised he agreed to this plan. I would have thought he would turn to salt at the very thought of public nudity, even in France."

"As a matter of fact," Fraser said wistfully, "the whole thing was his idea. Not many people know this but Sir Alistair is a nudist in his spare time."

"Well," sighed Cassie in resignation, "I suppose that's better than being a transvestite."

Fraser stood up and helped Cassie to her feet. "We have a lot of work to do," he said, "We'd better get started."

Two days later, Cassie was on a ferry from Dover to Calais. Once in France, she boarded a train to Paris then got lost in the maze that is the Gare du Nord. She eventually found the Metro which took her to another station and another train. After what seemed like an entire day of travelling, she arrived at Béziers and found a taxi to take her to Le Soleil d'Or. On the way, the driver kept looking at her in his mirror. Cassie was convinced he was undressing her with his eyes. It was quite late when they arrived at Le Soleil d'Or and Cassie was relieved that the few people who were about were wearing clothing because of the night air. She was shown to her accommodation – a small bungalow that was very similar to a Butlin's holiday chalet but without the charm. She slept fitfully – her mind full of thoughts about the next day.

============================

CHAPTER TWO

The management of Le Soleil d'Or thoughtfully provided new arrivals with a welcome basket of milk, orange juice, a few pieces of fruit, a couple of bread rolls, a little packet of marmalade and, most importantly, a small bottle of local wine. Cassie had not eaten since lunch the previous day and had a hearty breakfast. It was only when her desire for a cup of tea struck her that she realised that she would either have to do some grocery shopping or find somewhere that served hot meals. Those options would require a foray into the nudist colony and that was, after all, the reason she was there.

In anticipation of her imminent naked existence, Cassie had slept in the nude, something that was not an entirely new experience for her. After her breakfast, she had a lukewarm shower then wrapped a large towel around herself. She could hear people moving about outside but she was not yet ready to join them. She paused in front of the bathroom mirror – which was in dire need of a good polishing – and slowly let the towel slip to the floor. There she was – Cassie Pulaski, naked at nature intended.

It was, she decided, not such a bad sight. The breasts were small but firm with dark nipples. Her belly button was cuteness itself and the legs, though not very long, were those of a dancer. Only her feet disappointed her but who would be looking at feet in a nudist colony? With being looked at in mind, she decided her rather wild pubic hair could do with a trim but she forgot to bring scissors. The body would look even better with a tan and she was certainly in the right place to get one of those.

Cassie looked out the window and saw a bright and sunny summer's day. She also caught sight of several nudists going about their naked business. Some of them wore hats, others wore shoes, a few wore both. It was then that Cassie decided to slip on a pair of sandals. She had resigned herself to being naked but she refused to be barefoot as well. This was, to her, a matter of personal safety. Whether on a floor or on the ground, if there was a harmful object, her bare feet would invariably find it.

After another sip of wine and a couple of deep breaths, Cassie shoved some essentials – tissues, cigarettes, matches, money, keys – into a small brightly decorated cotton shoulder bag that had been handmade by a hippie friend of hers. She briefly wondered if she could position it to cover her privates then decided that would probably only draw attention. Cassie's mission was to blend in with her surroundings so she took another deep breath then opened the door and took a couple of very tentative steps outside.

The sun felt good on her body and there was just enough of a breeze to be pleasant. After a momentary pause, Cassie began to walk along the path in front of her. Soon the nervous walk turned into a more relaxed stroll as she explored the resort. Most of the accommodation was in bungalows similar to hers with each one set in its own little bit of grass interspersed with trees. The small path led to a larger path which took her into the centre of Le Soleil d'Or where larger buildings housed the main office, several small shops, a modest supermarket and – strangely for a nudist colony – a launderette. There was also a place to hire bicycles which Cassie thought might be handy. A short distance farther was some playing fields for volleyball, badminton, boules and mini-golf.

Unlike many nudist resorts, Le Soleil d'Or was not by the sea. Swimming was catered for in a huge L-shaped pool that was surrounded by a well-kept lawn filled with sunbeds. Cassie was beginning to think that a better name for Le Soleil d'Or would be The Garden of Eden.

Everywhere Cassie looked, there were naked people of all sizes, shapes and ages including children. Many of them smiled and greeted her as she passed and they did so without seeming to judge her in any way. If anything, they appeared more interested in making eye contact than in checking out her body. For her part, Cassie found it difficult to resist sneaking quick peeks at other people's attributes but she gradually became more accustomed to all the nudity, including her own. She was not exactly totally relaxed or completely uninhibited, but she felt capable of existing in this clothes-free environment, at least for a little while.

She decided to visit the supermarket and pick up a few provisions. Grocery shopping in the nude was a weird experience for her and she reflected that shopping in Sainsbury's back home in Ilford was never going to be quite the same again. By the time she returned to her bungalow – finding it again proved to be a small adventure of its own – she had been out for over an hour and a half. Time flies when one is having fun and naked.

As she sat on the small patio of her bungalow and devoured her simple lunch of cold ham on a freshly baked baguette, Cassie began to wonder how it would be possible to ever discover the identity of the Fox, assuming he or she was actually somewhere in Le Soleil d'Or. At first she thought that a process of elimination would be best, figuring that the Fox would probably be alone and thus removing all the couples and families from scrutiny. But if the Fox was as clever as she had been led to believe, it would certainly be possible that he or she was using a supposed partner as a cover, even one with children, which would certainly deflect any possible suspicion. So Cassie was back at square one. Like every detective she had ever seen in the movies, she would have to suspect everyone and hope that someone let slip a careless mistake or clue. As soon as lunch was finished, Cassie resumed her naked wanders in search of someone who seemed out of place.

Perhaps the Fox was a genuine nudist. It was entirely possible and would explain this unusual hiding place. For a secret agent to be so vulnerable by being naked seemed an odd decision. And yet that was exactly what Cassie was doing. That thought made her feel just a little bit more naked.

As she strolled around the grounds, Cassie became aware of the presence of various nationalities from around Europe. There were Germans and Dutch and Italians and even a few English as well as a fair number of French people. No one knew where the Fox was from originally so listening for a particular accent was not going to yield results. After a couple of fellow nudists had greeted Cassie with a cheerful "Bonjour" she realised there was another problem.

In their rush to recruit Cassie for this assignment, no one thought to ask if she was fluent in French. If they had, the answer would have been "not very". She had studied the language in school but absorbed very little from the lessons. Instead, she had picked up various words and phrases on holidays to France with her Aunt Connie, the aspiring beatnik. Even so, Cassie could understand written French much better than the spoken variety and her attempts to speak the language were usually greeted with bemused confusion.

Despite her linguistic shortcomings, Cassie was soon greeting just about everybody with a smiling "Bonjour" and passing quick judgment on them based on their response. To her relief, several replied to her in broken English which caused her to wonder how they knew she was English. Perhaps they thought she was Twiggy.

Cassie was beginning to recognise various people as she continued her wanderings around the site. There was Jean-Luc, the manager of Le Soleil d'Or, a short, rotund and amazingly hairless individual who always greeted her warmly. Cassie had initially tried to pump Marcel for information in broken French but learned very little other than Marcel was very partial to garlic. Another recurring face was a swarthy Italian who said nothing and kept to himself and spent a lot of time in the pool. There was a good looking Dutch chap who literally stuck out with a seemingly permanent erection.

Then there was a giggly gaggle of three gorgeous French girls who were slightly older than Cassie and seemed to be everywhere that she was. One of them in particular stood out, not because she was more gorgeous than her companions – she was not, even though she was tall and willowy with beautiful breasts and long straight black hair – but because she seemed to be taking as much notice of Cassie as Cassie was of her.

On the second day, Cassie caught sight of a figure lurking in the shadows. When he emerged, the first thing that Cassie noticed was that he was about forty, rather handsome in an old time movie sort of way, and had a disappointingly small penis. He was also the only person that Cassie had encountered who was actually paler than she was. She never heard him speak so she had no clue about his nationality. She nicknamed him the Ghost and put him at the top of her suspect list.

Another familiar and decidedly less suspicious person lived in a bungalow just a few yards away from Cassie's. He was old, at least sixty, with scraggly grey hair and a beard to match. He was also painfully thin and his wrinkly skin was so deeply tanned that it looked like leather. The old man spent most of his time sitting in a comfortable chair on his patio surrounded by several extremely lazy cats. It was difficult to tell if he was awake or not because he wore a pair of round wire-rimmed sunglasses. Cassie assumed he was French and a permanent resident of Le Soleil d'Or. They always smiled and said "Bonjour" as she passed but he seemed to take little interest in her nubile young body. The cats were even more apathetic. Their entire existence consisted of either lying on their backs in the sun or curled up asleep in the shade of the patio. Occasionally one of them would nestle onto the old man's lap to purr loudly as he endlessly stroked it. Cassie, a lifelong cat lover, found it all rather endearing and mentally bestowed the nickname of Catman on the old man.

On the afternoon of the second day, Cassie decided to take a short break from looking for clues, grabbed a towel and made her way to the swimming pool. She found an unoccupied sunbed, dropped her towel onto it, slipped off her shoes and immediately plunged into the very inviting water. She had never swum naked before and it was a sensual revelation to her entire body. Any inhibitions she had about being naked in that place completely disappeared in an instant. Everything was forgotten except for the sensations she was experiencing. She wanted to stay in the pool forever but she had never been a very strong swimmer so she reluctantly made her way to the ladder. Unfortunately, Cassie's exit from the pool was not as graceful as her motions when she was in it.

Ever since she was a little girl, Cassie possessed a clumsiness that was as endearing as it was inconvenient. She tripped coming out of the pool and virtually fell into the arms of the French girl with whom she had exchanged so many glances.

"Ça va?" the girl asked in a delicious accent.

"I'm okay," Cassie replied, more embarrassed than hurt as the girl helped her to her feet. Once she was standing, the girl seemed reluctant to let go of Cassie's hands so Cassie impulsively decided to pretend that she had hurt her ankle. "Ouch," she said.

"You are English?" the girl said with delight and obvious language skills. "Do you need a doctor?"

Cassie shook her head. "I'll be all right," she said in an affected weak voice. "I think I just need to walk it off"

The girl nodded as Cassie took a couple of tentative steps towards her sunbed. Once there, the girl finally let go of her hands and Cassie sat down heavily. She began to gently massage her supposedly injured ankle but this task was soon taken over by the girl who knelt in front of her with Cassie's foot in her lap.

"That is better?" the girl asked soothingly.

"Much," replied Cassie, enjoying the attention.

They smiled and exchanged looks. The girl gave Cassie the kind of look that Cassie had seen several times before. Although Cassie very much preferred men, she seemed to possess a certain something that greatly appealed to the followers of Sappho.

"My name is Simone," the girl almost whispered as she continued the look.

"Je m'appelle Cassie," replied Cassie, momentarily slipping into French for some weird unknown reason.

"Alors, Cassie," smiled Simone broadly, "what would you like to do now?"

"I think I should go back to my bungalow," said Cassie, trying her best to be practical.

"Eh bien," said Simone as she stood and offered her hand to Cassie, "I will walk with you."

As Cassie and Simone started to move off, Simone glanced back at her two companions who did not appear to be overly pleased but who simply shrugged and returned to their swimming. Cassie and Simone chatted about innocuous things as they walked and once or twice Cassie forgot that she was supposed to be limping. Once they arrived at the bungalow, Cassie felt it was only polite to invite Simone in for a cup of tea but she was not entirely sure that was a good idea.

Somehow the offer of a cup of tea turned into the more welcome suggestion of a glass of wine. Cassie had found a bottle of more than acceptable merlot in the site's supermarket and Simone appeared to approve of the selection. As Cassie sat with her foot propped up on a small coffee table, Simone took her glass and casually inspected the compact living area.

"It is funny, is it not?" Simone said in a quiet tone. "Your bungalow is exactly the same as ours and yet you have this all to yourself while I have to share mine with two others. It does not seem fair, does it?"

Cassie could only shrug in reply.

"The other two share the bed," Simone went on in between sips, "while I am confined to the sofa."

"That cannot be very comfortable," said Cassie, trying to sound sympathetic.

"Uncomfortable," sighed Simone, "and lonely."

"There must be bigger bungalows," Cassie said helpfully.

"Yes," replied Simone with another sigh. "But they are more expensive. Everything in Le Soleil d'Or is expensive. How can you afford this place on your own?"

"It's paid for," stammered Cassie, "by a friend."

"I see," Simone said with raised eyebrows. "And will this friend be joining you?"

"I don't know," replied Cassie, not certain how to answer, "Probably not."

Simone merely nodded and drained her glass. Cassie was jealous of her – not only of her luscious and very French body but also of her natural grace and elegance. There was something inherent in French women that made even the plainest of them seem sexy. But when they were gorgeous, as Simone undoubtedly was, it was awe inspiring. Cassie felt like a little lost girl in her presence. She got up to look for her cigarettes and suddenly found Simone next to her – very close to her.

"I should re-join my friends," Simone said without a flicker of emotion. "I hope we shall see each other again soon."

"I hope so too," Cassie mumbled in half a voice.

Simone leaned forward and kissed both her cheeks lightly, their breasts touching each other as she did so. Cassie was uncertain how to respond so did nothing. Simone gave her that look once more then moved to the door. Her body looked even more gorgeous in the glorious sunlight. They both paused on the patio and Simone briefly took Cassie's hand and squeezed it. An uncomfortable Cassie could only look down at Simone's pretty feet with their delicately painted toenails.

"Au revoir, Chérie," Simone said at last. Then she turned abruptly and strode away with an almost military gait rather than a feminine saunter. She passed by Catman who did not appear to notice her but then it was always difficult to tell if Catman was awake or asleep.

Cassie watched Simone until she was out of sight then went inside to resume her search for a cigarette. Once she found one and lit it, she returned to the open door and stood there, lazily leaning against the door jamb. She began to feel slightly guilty about neglecting her duties. Then she began to feel something else – the feeling of being watched. She glanced around nervously and thought she saw a figure in the shadows next to a nearby bungalow. She moved forward a couple of steps for a better view but the figure quickly disappeared.

It could have been anyone, she thought, or it could have been nothing. Her self-preservation instinct told her to go inside and close the door. But her newly found sense of duty forced her to carefully walk towards the spot. On the ground where she had seen the suspicious figure she found several crushed out cigarette ends. Someone had definitely been there and they had been there for a while. It was the sort of discovery that would do little to help Cassie sleep that night. She almost began to wish that she had invited Simone to share her bed. But then, did she really know who Simone was either?

==============================

CHAPTER THREE

After a somewhat disturbed night, Cassie was awakened by a persistent rapping on her door. She pulled herself out of the bed and looked around for her robe until she remembered that she did not really need it. She staggered to the door, which she had absent-mindedly left unlocked, and opened it to find Jean-Luc, the manager, with an envelope in his hand which he thrust towards her while mumbling "Bonjour" and looking at everything except her face. Cassie mumbled "Merci" in reply and quickly closed the door.

The envelope was addressed to her but she decided not to open it until she had peed, had a cigarette, and made a cup of coffee – not necessarily in that order. Once those important matters were taken care of, she settled into a wicker chair on the patio and carefully opened the envelope. It contained a small slip of paper on which was written in block letters: "I am in the village at La Boule d'Or, Uncle Silas."

Cassie nodded to herself as she recognised John Fraser's code name. She had been waiting for him to make some sort of contact and assumed he wanted a progress report. Going to the nearby village would mean wearing clothes. She had mixed emotions about that. While she had become quite accustomed to being naked, she had to admit that, in a strange way, she missed wearing knickers.

Of more immediate concern was the question of how to get to the village which was two or three miles away. Most of the nudists at Le Soleil d'Or had brought their own cars and some of them made occasional shopping trips in them but Cassie was reluctant to bum a ride with anyone because she felt it necessary not to advertise her movements. She considered walking but dismissed that idea after about ten seconds. Then she remembered there was a bicycle rental shop at the resort and that seemed to solve the problem – on the wild assumption that Cassie could remember how to ride a bike.

The bicycle shop was run by a tall, pipe-smoking gentleman who would have reminded Cassie of Jacques Tati if she had any idea who Jacques Tati was. He was, of course, naked with a body stained with bicycle grease but he was extremely friendly and helpful – at least to his female customers. He provided Cassie with a relatively safe three speed bike with a large basket on the handlebars. The transaction completed, Cassie elected to walk the bike back to her bungalow rather than risk her bare bum on the narrow and seemingly unforgiving saddle. She then put on a nice summer frock, some underwear, and a pair of flat sandals and set off on her journey.

The first hundred yards or so were somewhat unsteady but once Cassie had cleared the resort and was on the more or less level and thankfully traffic-free road, she pedalled along with something approaching confidence. Before she knew it, she was in the village and easily found La Boule d'Or on the main and virtually only street. It was a typically French country café with a well-stocked bar, half a dozen tables inside and a few outside, and several rooms for rent above. Cassie guessed the place dated back to the time of Napoleon and wondered why everything in the area seemed to be called golden. Cassie chained her bike to some railings and started to move towards the door of the café when a man seated at one of the outdoor tables reached out and grabbed her arm.

"Bonjour," said a familiar voice.

Cassie looked down and saw a completely different John Fraser than the one she had known in London. Instead of his well-tailored suit, he wore a loose-fitting pink polo shirt, a pair of denim shorts that revealed very hairy legs, and some leather Jesus boots on his not especially clean feet. The new image was completed by several days' growth of beard and a ridiculous straw trilby. Cassie was surprised the hat did not have a band saying "kiss me quick". She realised that Fraser was trying to blend in with his surroundings but she quickly formed the opinion that he had gone too far.

"What would you say to a bit of lunch?" Fraser asked with a twinkle in his slightly bloodshot eye.

"I would say," Cassie replied quietly as she sat at his table, "hello, lunch."

They shared a pleasant lunch with some not very serious conversation. Afterwards, Fraser invited Cassie up to his room where they were less likely to be overheard. It was a small and basic room with the usually garish French wallpaper clinging uncertainly to the walls. There was only one chair so they both sat on the edge of the bed. Unlike their time together in London, Cassie was relieved not to be naked with Fraser.

She gave him a quick summary of her activities since arriving at Le Soleil d'Or. As she did so, she realised how little there was to report other than the resort was filled with potentially suspicious characters. Fraser had not expected more. He knew it was going to take time for anyone, let alone an inexperienced operative, to even begin to bring the Fox out into the open. He did his best to reassure Cassie that she was doing a good job. She thought he was merely being kind.

"Are you still sure the Fox is there?" she asked.

"The information is good," said Fraser confidently. "The source is reliable. The operation would not have been approved otherwise. We just have to be patient – and very careful."

Cassie nodded as Fraser handed her a small card.

"Here is the telephone number for this place," he said. "Henri the owner will know where to find me. He moonlights as a police informant and thinks I'm from Interpol. Let me know if you find out anything. Until then, it's probably best that we don't meet – no need to draw attention to ourselves."

"All right," Cassie replied quietly.

He gave her an envelope with some additional cash and escorted her down the stairs. After checking that the coast was clear, he motioned for her to leave. She returned to her bike and began to pedal away without glancing backwards. It had been nice to see a familiar face – even if it was unshaven – but she now felt even lonelier than before.

Cassie decided to take advantage of being in the village to do a bit of shopping. In less than half an hour, she filled her handlebar basket with purchases from the local boucherie, boulangerie, pâtisserie and marchand de vin. If nothing else, she was going to eat and drink well on her adventure. She was tempted by a surprisingly chic little boutique but realised that she did not need clothes until she noticed a fabulous pair of bright red high-heeled sandals in the window. Fate was kind – they were exactly her size. After squeezing this last purchase into her basket, she returned to the café where Fraser was still sitting outside, two empty beer bottles on his table.

"What is it?" he asked anxiously. "What's wrong?"

"I need more money," Cassie replied calmly.

Cassie left the village feeling happier than when she arrived. The road back to Le Soleil d'Or was a typically rough French country road, not at all the sort a city girl like Cassie was used to. When an occasional car passed her, her little body tightened up nervously. The bike was now somewhat harder to control with the additional weight of her purchases. She found it difficult to pedal in a straight line and suddenly strayed off the side of the road onto a scattering of gravel, glass and other debris. She tried to apply the brakes but it was too late – she heard the unmistakable popping sound of the front tyre being punctured.

The bike could not be ridden and would only stand upright if Cassie supported it. She was less than halfway back to the resort and began to wonder if she could walk the bike the rest of the way. If she had been a religious person, she might have thought that God was punishing her for buying those sexy red shoes. Instead, she merely cursed her bad luck in language that few except for an ex-boyfriend or two would have thought her capable of. With no obvious solution in sight, she fell back on her usual reaction to a crisis – she lit a cigarette and stood there looking pathetic.

After about ten minutes, she heard the sound of a vehicle approaching from the direction of the village. It was a battered and partially decorated old Volkswagen bus with loud rock music blaring out of its open windows. It pulled over and stopped just a few feet from her. The side door slid open and out jumped a guy who could only be described as a hippie. Despite his hairy appearance, Cassie was very glad to see him.

"Bonjour, mademoiselle," he said in very bad French.

"Oh, thank God," Cassie all but screamed, "you're English!"

The hippie was quickly joined by the other occupants of the bus – another guy and two girls, all of whom were obviously dedicated followers of flower power. The two men approached Cassie while their girlfriends hung back by the bus.

"What's up, babe?" smiled the first guy, "Trouble with the old pushbike?"

"I've had a puncture," Cassie explained, her voice taking on an excessively posh tone for no apparent reason.

The hippie turned to his mate. "Have we still got that puncture repair kit, Pete?" he asked.

Pete shook his head. "We used it up on the spare back in Limoges."

"That's right," sighed the first hippie who then turned back to Cassie. "Where are you making for?"

"A place called Le Soleil d'Or," Cassie replied, the posh tone turning into one of hope. "It's a only mile or two up this road."

"Is that all?" beamed the hippie. "We can get you there, can't we, guys?"

"Sure," said Pete and the two girls nodded as well.

Without another word, the two men picked up the bike and carried it to the bus where they carefully placed it on top of a pile of backpacks, tents and sleeping bags. The two girls climbed in after it while their boyfriends resumed their seats in the front. Cassie hesitated a moment, then joined the girls in the back.

The two girls were about Cassie's age but their boyfriends seemed to be several years older although that could have been because of their beards. All four of them wore fairly dirty jeans. The boys wore tee-shirts while the girls had on flimsy loose-fitting tops with no bras underneath. One of the girls had dark curly hair styled into an Afro while the slimmer one had very long straight blonde hair that she constantly played with. Both of them wore excessive makeup and were barefoot.

"I'm Jenny," said the dark-haired one with a warm smile as she tried to make herself heard over the roar of the Rolling Stones, "and this is Hilary. The two geezers in the front are Gerry and Peter."

"Pleased to meet you," replied Cassie with genuine gratitude. "My name is Cassie."

"You're a long way from home, Cassie," said Gerry, turning down the tape deck to a less ear-splitting volume.

"I'm on holiday," shrugged Cassie.

"Holiday?" exclaimed Peter, "In the middle of bloody nowhere?"

"I like peace and quiet," said Cassie quietly.

"We don't," smiled Jenny. "We love nothing more than a good party, don't we, Hills?"

Hilary smiled in agreement.

"You're rather far from home yourselves," Cassie said, trying to make conversation. "Where are you headed?"

"That's a very good question, Cassie," said Gerry a bit flippantly. "And very good questions deserve very good answers. Unfortunately, I haven't got one."

"We're on a road trip," Hilary interjected in a low voice.

"Yes," nodded Jenny as she took out a cigarette and offered the pack to the other girls. "We've been travelling...what...five or six weeks now. Came across on the ferry and just took off. The original plan was to make our way through France and Spain and then on to Morocco."

"Morocco?" said Cassie, a bit surprised, "Why Morocco?"

"Why not?" asked Gerry.

"We plan to be gone about six months," explained Jenny, "then we'll go home and sign on the dole."

"If the van lasts that long," added Peter.

"How do you support yourselves?" Cassie asked as though she had never encountered free spirits before.

"We live off the land," said Gerry proudly.

"We take odd jobs here and there," replied Jenny, "sometimes for money, sometimes in exchange for food. We worked on a farm picking fruit for a couple of weeks."

"And there's always petty larceny," laughed Gerry.

Before Cassie could say anything else, the bus suddenly began to slow down.

"Is this the place?" Peter asked.

Cassie moved to look out the front window just in time to see the turning for Le Soleil d'Or.

"Yes, this is it," she said quickly.

"What sort of place is this?" asked Jenny with mild curiosity.

"It's a nudist colony," replied Cassie quietly.

"Cool!" said the two men in unison.

Cassie directed them to her bungalow and Peter was able to park reasonably close to it. For a minute or two, they simply sat there as everyone gazed out the window at the various naked bodies going by. Then Cassie began to move to collect the bags from the basket on the bike.

"I'm ever so grateful to you all," she said. "I don't think I could ever thank you enough. Would you be offended if I offered you a few francs?"

"Offended?" replied Gerry, "By money?"

"Tell you what," said Jenny quietly, "I would absolutely murder to have a real shower."

"Me too!" squeaked Hilary.

"Of course," replied Cassie awkwardly. "You must all come in for a while. But I warn you, it's nothing much."

"It's bigger than a tent, isn't it?" said Peter.

As the others prepared to get out of the bus, Gerry remained in his seat. "Hey, everybody," he said quietly, "this is a nudist colony, remember?"

The girls giggled a bit and everybody except Cassie began to remove their clothes. Once they were naked, the side door was opened, the two men took hold of the bike, and the five of them made a mad dash for the bungalow. Once inside, the four hippies collapsed in fits of laughter while Cassie tried to sort out her kitchen and make a pot of tea.

============================

CHAPTER FOUR

Nudity seemed to suit the hippies. The men with their long hair and beards looked like ancient Greeks while the two women displayed beautiful bodies decorated with strings of beads around their necks, wrists and ankles. None of them had any inhibitions and they had all obviously seen each other naked before but there was something about this situation that seemed different and a little bit exciting. For Cassie, it was a view into yet another world. She suddenly realised that she was still dressed and quickly slipped her clothes off. No one seemed to notice.

The bungalow seemed very small with five people in it. Jenny and Hilary had no trouble in locating the shower and emerged looking fresh and revived. Gerry and Peter, on the other hand, were content to lounge in the living area. It was not long before Cassie detected a burning aroma which she had encountered only once or twice before. Soon her four guests were passing a large joint back and forth among themselves as they sat in a semi-circle on the floor. Jenny motioned for her to join them and eventually Cassie came and sat next to Gerry. He handed her the joint and she tried to smoke it like a cigarette. The others laughed but Gerry patiently showed her how it was done. Cassie began to feel slightly strange and wondered why Fate had decided to puncture the tyre of her bicycle.

"We need music," said Hilary in a faraway voice as she began to dance around the room.

"I'm sorry," said Cassie, "I haven't got any."

"No music?" replied Jenny, "None at all?"

"I'll get some," said Peter as he rose and moved towards the door.

"Fetch my bag while you're at it," Gerry called after him.

Peter soon returned carrying a guitar and tossed a small leather bag to Gerry. Peter then perched on a chair and began to play evocative if somewhat repetitive music to which Hilary responded with a series of graceful movements. Jenny remained seated but swayed in time to the music before finally getting up and doing some dancing of her own. Most of it was for Gerry's benefit but he was too preoccupied with the contents of his bag. Cassie was left holding the joint and ended up putting it into the bungalow's only ashtray.

The music became slightly erratic as Hilary tried to get physical with Peter who was slow to respond. Jenny once again sat next to Gerry with Cassie on the other side of him.

"Well, girls," he chortled, "are we in the mood for a nice threesome?"

"Fuck you!" shouted Jenny as she stormed off to sit by herself on the other side of the room.

"No big deal," shrugged Gerry in a slurred voice. "I've got something better here anyway."

At first, Cassie thought he was referring to her, especially as he had been surreptitiously touching various parts of her body for the past half an hour. But instead, he continued to search through his bag before finally bringing out a couple of small pills.

"Want one?" he asked Cassie.

"What is it?" she asked.

"It's a surprise," he giggled.

"No, thanks."

Gerry smiled broadly then popped one of the pills into his mouth. He then closed his eyes and laid back on the floor, humming and mumbling to himself. By now, Peter had put down his guitar and he and Hilary had moved to the sofa where they were engaged in foreplay. Jenny sat in a corner chain-smoking cigarettes and possibly crying. She had somehow acquired a bottle of wine and was taking occasional sips from it without the benefit of a glass. Cassie was dazed and confused. It was still light outside so she decided to go for a walk in the hope that some fresh air might clear her head.

Everything seemed strange. She told herself that it was impossible for her to be high but she certainly was not normal. She did not stroll too far from the bungalow but kept slowly walking in a circle. At one point, she encountered the Ghost and noticed that he was a smoker.

"Stop watching me!" she shouted at him. He responded with a quick quizzical glance and continued on his way.

Cassie next found herself in front of Catman's bungalow. He was, as usual, on his patio with his three cats. She waved at him rather than calling out to him. It was then that Cassie realised that Catman was blind. What a concept, she thought – a blind nudist.

"Sorry," she called to him before returning to her own bungalow. Afraid of what she might find inside, she settled into one of the chairs on the patio and propped her feet up on the other. She was dying for a cigarette but had not thought to bring any with her. The sun was beginning to go down – the sky was filled with brilliant blue, orange and gold clouds that looked like a painting. Cassie saw them only briefly before drifting off to sleep.

It was quite dark when the chill of the night air caused Cassie to awaken. With half-opened eyes she stumbled to the door and went inside. The four hippies were more or less in the same places as when she left except now they were all deeply asleep. Two of them were snoring loudly – only one of whom was male. She crept across the room and made her way to the bedroom which was miraculously untouched. She quickly slipped into bed and felt her body melt into the mattress and pillows. In just a few minutes, she was asleep again.

When she awoke again, it was morning. Her guests had been up for a while, helping themselves to coffee and pastries. They greeted her warmly and without embarrassment. Only Gerry looked somewhat the worse for wear. Hilary handed Cassie a cup of black coffee which she only sipped. An open packet of cigarettes was lying on the kitchen counter and Cassie helped herself.

"Give us about an hour," Peter told her. "We'll have a wash and some breakfast and be on our way."

"You don't need to rush," Cassie replied.

"Yeah, we kind of do," said Peter sheepishly.

"I'll leave you to it then," Cassie shrugged. "I have to go and return my bike anyway."

"Can I go with you?" asked Jenny from across the room.

"Sure," said Cassie as she slipped on her sandals and picked up her shoulder bag. "You might want to put something on your feet as well."

"No need," replied Jenny. "I go barefoot all the time. The soles of my feet are like leather."

Luckily, the bike was still on the patio where it had been left the day before. The two women half walked and half carried it back to the rental shop. The owner was not as cheerful as before and charged Cassie extra both for the puncture and for keeping the bike overnight. Cassie hoped this would not affect any possible future rentals.

Once the bike was disposed of, they were able to stroll more freely around the resort. Jenny seemed quite fascinated by it all and many of the nudists found her a bit unusual as well with her Afro and multi-coloured beads. At one point, they passed Simone and her two girlfriends. Polite greetings were exchanged but Simone gave Jenny an icy stare while barely giving Cassie a second glance.

"I see they have lezzies here as well," Jenny commented when they were a few yards away.

"They're probably just good friends," suggested Cassie.

"Not that there's anything wrong with that," mused Jenny. "Have you ever, you know, experimented?"

"No," Cassie lied.

"I have," Jenny said somewhat matter-of-factly. "About two weeks ago, Hilary and I were in the back of the bus. We had been driving for hours and we were bored and had a little too much wine. We started to kiss and touch each other. It was nice. But then the boys saw what was going on and wanted to watch. We stopped and never did again. In fact, Hilary has never mentioned it."

"Do you think you'll ever try it again?" asked a very curious Cassie.

"I don't know," replied Jenny wistfully. "Gerry keeps me pretty happy that way. If I did, it would probably be with someone small and delicate - maybe a Japanese girl. They're like little porcelain dolls, aren't they?"

"I suppose so," shrugged Cassie.

"Of course," said Jenny slowly, "you fall pretty much into the small and delicate category yourself."

Cassie's only response was to blush.

"Can I ask you a serious question?" Jenny asked, stopping in the shade of a large tree. "What is a girl like you doing in a place like this all on your own?"

"To tell you the truth," Cassie answered after a moment's hesitation, "I'm a spy on a secret mission."

"All right," laughed Jenny loudly. "Forgive me for not minding my own bloody business."

As the two women paused to light a pair of cigarettes, Cassie noticed the approach of Jean-Luc. He spoke in very quick French to Cassie while stealing sidelong glances at Jenny's rather delicious body. From what Cassie could understand, Jean-Luc was aware of her overnight guests and was miffed at not being informed of their presence.

"It was only for one night," Cassie tried to explain, raising her voice as if it would assist in the translation. "They are passing through, on their way to somewhere else."

The Frenchman's rant continued and Cassie was fairly certain she heard something about extra charges.

"Put it on my bill," she finally said as if money did not matter to her and turned away from him.

When they returned to the bungalow, Gerry and Peter were waiting by the bus and Hilary was in animated conversation with Catman on his patio. When she saw Cassie and Jenny, she gave Catman a quick kiss on the cheek and rushed back to her friends.

"That blind geezer is really cool," Hilary said with very bright eyes. "He says that I'm beautiful."

"How would he know?" asked Peter.

"He knows," replied Hilary mysteriously.

The four hippies took turns giving Cassie a goodbye kiss. Some were more intense than others and a couple involved a firm embrace. Then they all climbed into the bus and, after a couple of false starts, the engine noisily came to life. As they slowly backed out of their parking space, Cassie felt both sad and relieved to see them go. She would think about them often in the days ahead, wondering where they were and what they were doing. She seemed to envy the excitement in their lives while reflecting that being an undercover spy was not all that she had expected. Still, she had not done much spying lately and she resolved to avoid further distractions and to concentrate on her assignment. The only unanswered question that remained was – how?

================================

CHAPTER FIVE

Cassie realised that she was never going to discover anything from inside her bungalow. The Fox was out there somewhere and he or she was just as naked as Cassie was, only more dangerous. There were several hundred naked people at Le Soleil d'Or and virtually all of them had to be considered as suspects. It was going to be up to Cassie to somehow narrow the list. At the moment, her usual thinking aids of coffee and cigarettes were not helping very much. She decided a walk in the fresh air – because the bungalow still smelt slightly of hippies – might be beneficial.

It was a somewhat cloudy day but still warm enough to be naked. One person Cassie could easily remove from the suspect list was old Catman who seldom seemed to leave the security of his patio. As she passed by his bungalow, Cassie called out her usual cheerful "Bonjour", practically the only French word she felt confident using.

"Your friends have gone?" he replied in a loud if somewhat raspy voice.

Cassie was surprised to be actually be engaged in conversation with him and moved closer. "Yes," she said. "They were just passing through."

"Pity," he sighed. "You must be lonely on your own."

"And you," Cassie replied in an uncertain tone.

"I have my cats," smiled Catman.

By now Cassie was standing next to him on the patio while a white cat with black splotches sniffed and purred around her ankles.

"My name is Armand," the old fellow said, extending a hand of friendship.

"I'm Cassie," she replied, taking his hand which he seemed reluctant to release. "You speak very good English."

"And you speak very bad French," he said with a smile. "I speak several languages. They are among my hobbies."

"Do you have many hobbies?" Cassie asked politely.

"Yes," nodded Armand gravely, "too many."

"Which is your favourite?"

"People."

He still held her hand and now he gently placed it against his cheek. Cassie sensed there was something almost pagan, something very earthy, about the old man and she found it strangely comforting.

"Are you naked?" he asked after a long pause.

"Yes, of course," she replied in a whisper.

"It is good to be naked, is it not?" he smiled.

Cassie half expected him to feel her body as she thought he must have done with Hilary but he simply sat there the way he always did.

"You were going somewhere," he said calmly. "You must not let me keep you."

"It's been a pleasure," replied Cassie, searching for the right words, "talking to you."

"Whenever you wish," Armand smiled as a ginger cat leapt into his lap. "I am always here, as you know."

For some reason, Cassie felt compelled to give the old man a kiss on the cheek before she continued on her way. Her thoughts then returned to her secret assignment. She wondered what John Fraser would do in her situation. Not a lot, she decided. He had not really been much help so far.

Her stroll brought her down to the centre of the resort and she noticed a youngish couple at the office – still fully dressed – who were checking in. A sudden thought struck Cassie. What if Sir Alistair's information was faulty? What if the Fox was indeed coming to Le Soleil d'Or but had not arrived yet? Or, even worse, what if he had been there but already left. Cassie was convinced there might be vital clues in the office register. Even assuming the Fox was using a fake name, something important might be revealed by looking carefully through the register. That was, of course, unlikely to happen. Cassie was not exactly on the best terms with Jean-Luc and she could not imagine him giving her any sort of access to his files.

Cassie wondered if it would be possible to break into the office at night to either examine the register or simply steal it. That would be a real act of espionage. The only problem was that Cassie lacked the necessary skills for breaking and entering. Her education in criminal activity was sadly deficient.

There was a small roundabout not far from the office where several of the resort's small roads converged. In the middle was a single flagpole from which the French tricolour proudly flew. On one corner of the roundabout was a little café that served coffee and ice cream. Sitting outside at one of its tables with a wickedly indulgent chocolate sundae was an ideal location for people watching.

Everyone seemed to pass by this point sooner or later. Cassie's mind started to wander as she idly watched the parade of flesh. She wondered why fat people would want to be nudists. She was puzzled by families of nudists. Theoretically, it seemed a healthy pursuit but how did the children actually feel about it? Cassie knew that she would feel uncomfortable being naked in front of her mother or her Aunt Connie and she certainly never had any desire to see them in the nude. And why did people from warm places like Spain or Italy choose to come to France for a holiday? Was it just to get naked?

Cassie could remember her holidays on the continent with her bohemian Aunt Connie, back in the days before the explosion of tourism. There were villages that they passed through in the old Morris Minor where foreigners were still a novelty. Places she remembered as sleepy fishing villages now had large beaches lined with tall hotels. At least Le Soleil d'Or was reassuringly old-fashioned. Cassie was so wrapped up in nostalgia that she forgot she was naked – until a cold drip of chocolate ice cream landed on her belly. She caught it with her finger which she licked as she returned to reality.

"Do you mind if I join you?"

Cassie turned and came face to face with the small penis of the Ghost. Looking up, she saw that he was smiling politely and holding a large bowl of rich French coffee, the aroma of which was intoxicating. Cassie was delighted at the prospect of interviewing a prime suspect although he was hardly her first choice for a companion.

"I'm sorry if I seemed to be stalking you," he said in a slightly halting voice, "but you're one of the few single people here and, of course, you're English."

The Ghost was English too. His name was Nigel and he was an estate agent from Crewkerne in Somerset. He was approaching middle age although he was one of those people who seemed to have been middle-aged all his adult life. Having finally found someone who would listen, he proceeded to tell Cassie his life story which seemed to be a tale hardly worth telling. This was his first time at a nudist resort although he had been a home nudist for many years. He decided it was time to take the plunge although his wife was less than happy about the decision.

"Anita doesn't like nudity," he explained quietly. "She's not a prude, not exactly, it's just that she is uncomfortable about bodies, including her own. She doesn't have a bad body, just not a great one."

"Presumably you left her back in Somerset," said Cassie with very mild interest.

"No," replied Nigel solemnly, "she's in the bungalow. I told her before we came that she wouldn't have to be, well, nude – that she could wear a swimsuit or something when we went out. But the other people didn't like that. They gave her dirty looks and told her to strip. So now she just stays in the bungalow and we still have another week of holiday to go."

"I sympathise," said Cassie soothingly, "but obviously this sort of place is not for everyone."

"I love it here," Nigel said, almost to himself. "I love being naked."

It was clear that neither Nigel nor his very inhibited wife was the Fox. Cassie was anxious to bring the conversation to a conclusion but Nigel seemed in no hurry to go anywhere. If anything, there were little clues that he was finding his chat with Cassie to be somewhat stimulating. Cassie had finished her ice cream and lit a cigarette.

"Well," she said as she exhaled a large cloud of smoke just to the left of him, "I wish you lots of luck with everything."

"In point of fact," Nigel stammered without looking at her, "I was hoping we might be, well, friends – you know, companions who do things together."

"I don't think so," said Cassie as she rose to leave.

"I think your body is wonderful," he called after her, his eyes fixed on her bouncing bum.

"Yes, babe," she replied over her shoulder, "and yours is a wasteland."

In her haste to put some distance between herself and Nigel, Cassie found herself at the recreation grounds. There were all sorts of physically fit suspects there to be investigated. Cassie was most suspicious of those with obvious tan lines from bikinis and swimsuits. They were clearly not dedicated nudists or perhaps merely recent arrivals. Either way, it was logical to think that the Fox would be reasonably athletic if he or she was a typical secret agent. As Cassie gazed at the two dozen or so people involved in various activities, she concluded that there was not one of them she had any hope of ever beating in a confrontation.

After a minute or two, Cassie noticed Simone and several other very healthy women warming up next to the volleyball court. She wandered over to them and was greeted with a big smile and a hug.

"Bonjour, Chérie," Simone practically sang to her.

"Hello," replied Cassie, momentarily caught off guard.

"Have you come to play?" asked Simone brightly. "We are about to begin a volleyball match. It is the girls against the boys. Will you join us in showing them who is superior?"

Cassie hesitated. She had never played volleyball in her life but it seemed a good opportunity to observe people without seeming suspicious.

"Come on," said Simone's red-headed friend with breathless enthusiasm. "It will be fun. We distract the boys with our bouncing doudounes and have a good laugh at their bouncing popols."

"Yes," replied Cassie, glancing down at her baby breasts, "that does sound like fun."

A few minutes later, Cassie was in the midst of the action. She had absolutely no idea of the rules of the game or the scoring system and she had so far not even touched the ball. The other women were darting and jumping everywhere and she watched the ways they were hitting the ball while at the same time trying not to get in their way. She barely noticed the assembly of male nudity on the other side of the net. She did her best to hit the ball when it came near her but one of the other girls invariably got to it before her. Cassie was getting a lot of exercise without really accomplishing anything. But the rest of her team were squealing with delight and constantly patting each other on the bottom. After a while, a whistle blew and, much to Cassie's relief, everything stopped.

"Did we win?" she asked Simone.

"We destroyed them," replied Simone triumphantly. "They are dust beneath our feet."

"I must love and leave you, Chérie," she said with a slight smile. "I have things to do today."

"What sort of things?" Cassie asked with only mild interest.

"Things," shrugged Simone.

"No rest for the wicked," said Cassie with a little laugh.

"So I am told," replied Simone with another sigh.

They shared a kiss then Simone gathered up her clothes, tucked them under her arm and left, leaving the door open. Cassie watched her disappear down the path then stood there listening to the birds singing in the trees around her. It was going to be another beautiful day. She then had a sudden urge to clean her teeth for the second time that morning.

Cassie fussed obsessively with her makeup and hair then put on a simple gold necklace and a pair of heart-shaped ear studs, She slipped on her sandals but quickly exchanged them for her red heels. She wanted to feel dressed up – in a nudist sort of way – when she went out. She was not sure where she was going but she definitely felt she had to be doing something.

"Bonjour, Armand!" she called out, deciding to pay the old man a brief visit.

"You are very happy this morning," he replied with a strange twinkle in his blind eye.

"How can you tell?" asked Cassie.

"The lightness of your step," Armand said as though he were some sort of mystic, "and the tone of your voice. You are not only happy but satisfied."

"Very satisfied," nodded Cassie.

Cassie looked over at the muscular men and saw nothing but limp defeat. She could not imagine any of them being the Fox. Everyone moved to the side lines where there were plastic cups of iced water and big fluffy towels for mopping up sweat. Cassie felt slightly guilty helping herself to both. The water was refreshing but it was difficult for her to find sufficient energy to use the towel.

"How are you?" Simone asked, looking just as bright and fresh as before the game.

"I'm knackered," sighed Cassie.

Simone smiled and took the towel from her and began to give her a thorough drying off. As she did so, their bodies came closer and closer together until Cassie thought that Simone was going to plant a kiss on her.

"I'm not like that, you know," Cassie whispered as Simone mopped the sweat from her face.

"Yes, you are," replied Simone simply. "All women are. You just do not know it yet."

Cassie wanted to change the subject. "I need a shower," she said.

"We all do," laughed Simone. "We are going to the big ablutions hut to shower all together."

"Together?" replied Cassie as unpleasant memories of secondary school suddenly filled her head.

"Why not?" said Simone as she linked arms with both Cassie and the redhead. "We have nothing to hide."

The shower was welcome even if the giggling company was not necessarily to Cassie's suburban English taste. The women seemed to talk all at once and in French so

Cassie felt slightly isolated. She was surprised that, once in the shower, Simone did not seem to be paying any attention to her at all but was instead frolicking with the two girls she shared a bungalow with. Cassie was the first to leave the shower. She found her sandals and shoulder bag and picked up a towel which she put around her shoulders. Then she began to walk swiftly along the path back to her bungalow. She quickly entered and closed the door quietly with a large sigh of relief.

She had narrowed the list of suspects down very slightly. At this rate, it was going to take her months to investigate every likely candidate. For the first time, she seriously considered giving the whole project up. People were counting on her and she was beginning to fear that trust may have been misplaced. She wished she had inherited a few spy genes from her parents. No doubt Mum would know exactly what to do but Cassie was lost and confused. She needed a plan and organising her thoughts had never been one of her strengths.

The other thing was that she was no longer certain that she wanted to be naked all the time. She was constantly seeing other bodies that were more developed and voluptuous than hers and it was beginning to affect her self-confidence. She had always been relatively happy with her slightly boyish body and elfin looks but now it only seemed to appeal to lesbians, estate agents and stoned hippies. She wanted a change of image but how could anyone change their image when they are naked? The only thing she could think of was to trade in her old sandals for those new red high heels. Now they were sexy!

===========================

CHAPTER SIX

Cassie did not usually wander out after dark but she decided that the shadows of the night might be a good place to look for suspects. Like most nudists, she put on some clothes after the sun went down, in this case a skirt and top and those sexy red shoes. She never wore a bra but she debated with herself about wearing knickers. In the end she settled on a pair of red bikini briefs that nearly matched the colour of her shoes. Feeling slightly risqué and naughty, she ventured out onto the badly lit paths of Le Soleil d'Or.

She soon became aware of the sound of loud music. On Friday and Saturday nights during the summer, the resort offered free entertainment on a small stage next to the recreation area. It usually consisted of local talent anxious to strut their stuff in front of a fairly undemanding audience. The stage faced an expanse of lawn on which the holidaymakers could try to make themselves comfortable while imbibing their favourite beverages and being eaten alive by mosquitos. In the absence of any televisions in Le Soleil d'Or, it was for most the only alternative to reading a book or having sex.

The performances never contained nudity, although that might have helped some of the acts, especially a smiling magician and his lovely assistant. His tricks had a fifty percent success rate and the audience was soon wishing he would make himself disappear. He was followed by a small group of preteen girls from a dance school who had travelled all the way from Toulouse to perform basic choreography to recorded music. This was the performance that was in progress when Cassie arrived.

She was tempted to quietly withdraw when a tall and intense chap of about thirty strode purposefully onto the stage with a guitar in one hand and a wooden stool in the other. Without any sort of introduction, he perched on his stool near the edge of the stage and began to strum his guitar like a professional. The crowd fell very quiet as he became to sing in a sweet voice with rough edges. It was an old Russian song called "Moscow Nights" and he sang it in what sounded like perfect Russian. There was a brief pause when he finished and then the audience burst into loud and appreciative applause. The singer bowed once then took his guitar and stool and rushed offstage. There were a few calls for an encore but the singer was gone.

Cassie was very impressed by his performance but even more intrigued by the presence of an apparently Russian singer in the middle of France. This was the Cold War, after all – the Iron Curtain was still firmly in place. Cassie moved to the area behind the stage but there was no sign of the mystery singer. She did locate a member of the resort staff who confirmed that the singer was not one of their usual local performers and that all he knew about him was that his name was Ivan. Cassie wished she had taken of photo of him but she had no camera. She had asked for one before leaving London – an essential bit of spy equipment, she thought – but she was told that cameras were not appreciated in nudist colonies. She could only hope to remember his description: tall, blonde and very good looking. She was certain she would recognise him if she saw him again.

The next act – a pair of mimes – was very anti-climactic so Cassie decided to go to her favourite café for an ice cream. The waiter remembered her from previous visits and conversed with her in English. When he had gone, a young chap at the next table leaned back in his chair towards her.

"I really love your accent," he said in an unmistakable American voice. "Where are you from, doll?"

"I should have thought that was obvious," Cassie replied coolly. "I'm from England."

"What part?"

"All of me."

It was an old joke but Cassie saw little point in wasting wit on this callow youth. He was young, no more than twenty-one, and seemed to be the embodiment of what Americans referred to as the Joe College look – nice features, neatly trimmed brown hair, expensive yet casual clothing, and an easy manner that suggested a privileged upbringing. His companion was the same age and quite different in almost every respect with his black unruly mop of hair, horn-rimmed glasses on a prominent nose, and a nervousness that he would probably never get over. Their youth had the effect of making Cassie feel older than she actually was.

"Naw," said Joe College with a small laugh, "I meant: are you staying here?"

"Yes," said Cassie succinctly.

"Cool!" he replied. "So are we."

"I wouldn't have thought they see many Americans here," Cassie said, trying to unnerve the one with glasses with a semi-sultry stare.

"And they ain't gonna see many more at these prices," laughed Joe College. "My name is Biff, by the way, and this is Lester."

"Biff?"

"It's a nickname."

"I should hope so," sighed Cassie.

"And you are?" prodded Biff.

"My name is Cassie," she replied with unnecessary haughtiness, "Cassie Pulaski."

"Pulaski?" exclaimed Biff. "That doesn't sound like no limey name."

"My father was an American," Cassie said reluctantly.

"Really," replied Biff with genuine interest. "Where from?"

"I don't know," Cassie said in a quiet voice. "He died before I was born – in the war, you know."

"Sorry," said a slightly subdued Biff. "Have you ever been to America?"

"No," replied Cassie, "at least, not yet."

"I'd love to go to England someday," gushed Biff to what he perceived to be a captive audience. "There's so much good stuff there – you know, land of the Beatles and all that. Tell me something, are all the English girls as sexy as you?"

"No," smiled Cassie in spite of herself. "I'm the only one."

Cassie's ice cream arrived and she turned away from the boys to concentrate on it. But Biff was not so easily discouraged despite the silent protests of his companion. For her part, Cassie was now more interested in her chocolate ice cream even though it made her feel chilly and caused her nipples to stand erect.

"We just got here a few hours ago," Biff continued. "We're on vacation. We both go to Columbia University in New York. I'm a history major and Lester is studying political science. We thought it would be fun to hitch hike around Europe for a few weeks. There are so many old places, not like in the States. And, of course, there are the foxy European girls."

Lester finally spoke for the first time. "A truck driver told us about this place," he said in a loud mumble. "We thought it was just a campsite – you know, a place to pitch our tent for a couple of nights."

"I didn't know they allowed tents here," said Cassie.

"Oh, yeah," Biff chimed in. "There's a whole field set aside for campers."

"Interesting," said Cassie to herself.

"So is it true?" Biff asked. "Is this really a nudist colony?"

"Yes, it is," smiled Cassie at Lester's uncomfortable expression. "In fact, nudity is obligatory during daylight hours."

"Wow!" enthused Biff. "That sounds like fun. And you're a nudist, right?" Cassie simply nodded. "Wow – really looking forward to tomorrow."

"Well, boys," said Cassie as she rose from the table with her ice cream only half consumed, "as the saying goes – don't call me, I'll call you."

She started to walk away and was relieved the boys had not decided to follow her.

"By the way," Biff called after her in a typically loud voice, "I really love your shoes!"

The next morning, naked Cassie decided to go exploring. She followed the perimeter of Le Soleil d'Or and, after a couple of wrong turns, came upon the resort's modestly sized campsite. It was basically a field on which were pitched about a dozen tents, several parked cars, and a couple of small caravans. To one side, were a pair of small ablutions huts, each with a shower unit for one person – or two people who knew each other very well – and a dreaded continental-style stand-up toilet. Cassie had a quick wander around the field. Most of the tents were empty but obviously in use. There was no sign of the two Americans from the night before.

She left the field and took a different return route that brought her into the main square. There was a small crowd of people gathered, including the ubiquitous Simone, and two gendarmes outside the office, one of whom was talking to Jean-Luc while the other – on his first visit to Le Soleil – was taking in as much of the scenery as he could. Simone saw Cassie and moved to greet her.

"Whatever has happened here?" Cassie asked anxiously.

"Someone broke into the office last night," Simone replied like a reliable reporter. "It is all very strange. The only thing they took was the registration book."

"You mean the one of people checking in?" asked Cassie with some amazement.

"So it would seem," shrugged Simone. "They did not touch the money box or any of the other papers, just that book. Jean-Luc is furious."

Cassie did not bother to ask why. If she had thought about stealing the book to look for clues about the Fox, perhaps the Fox suspected that there was an undercover agent in the resort and had the same idea. If that was the case then the Fox was becoming a hunter as well as the hunted and Cassie was beginning to feel a little bit like a possible sitting duck. She immediately went to the public phone box outside the supermarket and rang the number of La Boule d'Or in the village. The barman of the café had limited knowledge of English and Cassie realised that she had no idea what pseudonym Fraser was using. She kept repeating "Interpol, Interpol" before hanging up in frustration.

The gendarmes left and the crowd dispersed. Jean-Luc went back inside the office where he continued to shout and swear at no one in particular. Cassie carelessly stepped into the road and was narrowly missed by a passing car. She muttered something nasty about the driver and made a mental note of the number plate. She then stopped short as a new idea occurred to her.

"Number plate..." she whispered to herself.

Cassie turned just in time to catch sight of Biff and Lester emerging from the supermarket that was more market than super. They were naked and each carried a paper bag. Biff wore a baseball cap and a pair of gleaming white tennis shoes while Lester had on some well-used black and white sneakers. The only parts of their bodies that were tanned were their faces and arms. Cassie found it interesting that Lester, the shy and submissive one, had a much larger penis than Biff. She thought it must have been an interesting experience that morning when the two boys saw each other naked for the first time. She could only wonder what their reaction would be to seeing her.

"Hey, guys!" she called out when it became apparent they had not noticed her.

They all moved closer together with two of them smiling broadly and one of them looking embarrassed. The Americans seemed momentarily speechless as they each, in their own way, conducted a visual tour of her nubile body.

"I almost didn't recognize you without your red shoes," said Biff with a quick downward glance at her sandals. "This place is something else, isn't it?"

"So you like being nudists?" Cassie asked cheekily.

"I think it's great," Biff replied enthusiastically, "but it took me half an hour to talk Les into getting out of the tent."

The three of them began to walk slowly in the direction of the campsite with Cassie in the middle. She had noticed that the boys were very careful not to accidentally touch or bump into each other but neither seemed to mind the slightest bit of contact with her. They soon arrived at their tent and Biff invited Cassie to join them inside.

"It's roomy, isn't it?" she commented politely.

"Well," shrugged Biff, "we had been hoping to entertain along the way but, so far, no luck."

"You're our first visitor," added Lester.

There was just enough room for the three of them to sit cross-legged with their heads touching the canvas. A bit of physical contact was hard to avoid. Cassie could never understand the appeal of tents but she had other things on her mind. She was probably about to break several rules in the spy's rulebook as she considered involving the boys in her mission.

"Can I ask you a weird question?" she inquired.

"Those are the best kind," replied Biff.

"Can I see your passports?" she asked.

Biff and Lester looked at each quizzically then shrugged and began to rifle through their backpacks. They soon produced the passports and handed them to Cassie. The passports were quite new – only issued a couple of months previously – and the only entry in them was the visa and stamp of their arrival in France ten days ago. Cassie also discovered Biff's real name and decided to keep calling him Biff. Satisfied that they were legitimate, she handed the passports back and leaned forward like some sort of conspirator.

"How would you boys like to earn a few francs?" she asked in a hushed voice.

"Well," shrugged Biff, "we don't really need any extra dough. My dad is bankrolling this whole trip. But if you want a favour, just ask."

"All right then," Cassie replied, feeling slightly more assured, "how would you like to help me with a little project?"

"What kind of project?" Lester asked.

"I want to make a list of the number plates of all the vehicles in Le Soleil d'Or and what country they come from," Cassie said quickly in what seemed like a single breath.

Biff and Lester looked at each other for a moment and then back at Cassie. Lester was absent-mindedly covering his privates and Biff had obviously been hoping for something more exciting or possibly even personal.

"The obvious question," Biff finally said, "is why?"

"I can't tell you that," Cassie replied quietly.

Again the boys exchanged looks. Lester was frowning but Biff seemed bemused.

"Why the hell not?" said Biff with a laugh. "The only thing we had planned to do today was play miniature golf and look at all the girls. I guess we'll still be able to look at the girls in between doing this."

"Thank you so much," gushed Cassie. "We can get some pens and paper from the card shop."

Cassie led the way out of the tent and down to the shops. Once they had obtained their supplies, they stood in front of a wall on which was a large map of the resort.

"I think it would be most efficient if we split up and did different parts of the site," Cassie said. "When we're finished, we'll meet at the ice cream shop."

"Sounds good to me," said Biff who liked to think he was the sort of guy who was up for anything. "Just tell me one thing."

"What's that?" asked Cassie nervously.

"There is a good reason for this, isn't there?"

"Oh, yes," replied Cassie, "a very good reason."

The three of them went their separate way but not before Cassie had impulsively planted a kiss on each of them. Most people in the resort seemed to pay little or no attention to their strange activity – with the possible exception of the one person whose curiosity Cassie had hoped not to arouse.

===========================

CHAPTER SEVEN

After their well-deserved ice cream treats, Cassie and the two Americans made their way to her bungalow with the results of their survey. Cassie was surprised to find John Fraser waiting for her – sitting comfortably on the patio and naked except for his straw hat, sunglasses and Jesus boots. He did not move as the youthful trio approached him. Cassie felt mildly embarrassed but the two boys were filled with curiosity.

"Who is this?" Biff asked in a smart aleck voice, "Your sugar daddy?"

"Not exactly," Cassie replied quietly.

Fraser finally stood up as Cassie came onto the patio. She had never seen him naked before and had mixed feelings about seeing it all now. Biff and Lester hung back, trying to assess the situation.

"I heard you wanted to see me," Fraser said.

"Yes," said Cassie, barely audible.

Fraser turned his attention to the Americans. "You gentlemen will please excuse us," he said with a voice that sounded like authority. "Cassie and I need to have a private chat."

"Yeah, okay," mumbled Biff.

The boys handed Cassie their papers but seldom took their eyes off the imposing figure of Fraser. Biff turned to leave but Lester did not move.

"I wonder," Lester stammered, "if I could please use your bathroom."

Fraser almost laughed and Biff looked up to heaven. After a quick nod from Cassie, Lester quickly disappeared inside the bungalow.

"He's very fussy about toilets," Biff struggled to explain. "He has real problems with these French squatty ones."

After a couple of minutes, Lester returned and the boys took off down the path to the campsite. Cassie was filled with uncertainty about Fraser's presence in the resort. She thought that the reason she was there was because Fraser and the other agents might be recognised by the Fox.

"We better go inside," Fraser said, motioning for Cassie to enter before him. It was also the first time that Fraser had seen Cassie naked and he had to admit that he was pleasantly impressed. But he was less happy to see her on apparently friendly terms with a pair of strangers.

"Who are your friends?" he asked sharply.

"Just a couple of boys I met," Cassie said like a child answering a parent. "They're American college kids – much too young to be the Fox."

"The Fox is not necessarily working alone," Fraser said.

"Unlike me," Cassie whispered to herself.

Cassie went into the kitchen and poured herself a glass of mineral water. She would have offered one to Fraser but she knew he preferred more potent beverages. He came and stood very close to her and, for a moment, Cassie thought he was going to take her into his athletic arms. She decided to defuse the possibility.

"That's an interesting scar," she said, pointing to a long mark on the upper left side of his chest.

Fraser laughed slightly. "That's a kind of war wound," he said, stepping back slightly. "I got that fighting for a lady's honour. Apparently, she wanted to keep it."

Cassie laughed lightly and mood seemed to become marginally less tense. But then Fraser's face took on a more serious expression.

"I thought you had some sort of emergency," he said with a touch of irritation.

"I did," replied Cassie defensively. "The main office was broken into last night. The only thing taken was the register."

"So?"

"I thought about taking the register to look for clues about the Fox," Cassie went on in a strong voice. "Maybe the Fox had the same idea about looking for clues about me – if he had any reason to suspect that I'm here."

"That's good," said Fraser thoughtfully. "Whatever you're doing must be worrying him."

"Enough to make him want to do something about it?" asked Cassie.

"Only as a last resort," replied Fraser. "He won't want to do anything to jeopardize his mission."

"I had an idea," Cassie said excitedly. "I thought of a way we might track him down. We've made a list of all the number plates of all the cars at Le Soleil d'Or. You could check them out and see if one of them looks suspicious."

She handed Fraser the papers that she and her friends had compiled. He gave them a cursory glance and then shook his head.

"It's going to take a long time to go through all these numbers," he said, "especially with so many different countries."

"Doesn't Counter Intelligence have some sort of computer for that kind of thing?" Cassie asked with the innocence of youth.

"No," laughed Fraser, "they can't afford them."

"Well, what am I supposed to do?" Cassie almost cried.

"Just keep doing what you've been doing," replied Fraser calmly. "And for God's sake, relax. You really need to get laid. Meaningless sex is an integral part of being a spy. It's one of the main motivations for the job."

"Thanks," said Cassie in half a voice, "that's an incredibly big help."

"No one said this job would be easy," sighed Fraser, "or even successful."

"So I just keep doing what I've been doing and hope the Fox doesn't decide to kill me," said Cassie with a tear or two forming.

"You have to understand," Fraser said in a suddenly stern voice. "You are expendable. Your job is to flush the Fox out. If the only way you can do that is by getting killed, the department is willing to pay that price."

"And what if I decide to quit?" Cassie all but screamed.

"Then you'll find it very difficult to get back into the UK," Fraser replied coldly.

Cassie lashed out and struck his face. "You're a bastard!" she cried.

"I'm afraid that's one of the requirements for the job," he said quietly.

"Get out," Cassie sobbed.

"I'm going," Fraser replied. "I won't expect to hear from you again until you have better news."

Cassie heard the door close but could see nothing through her tears. She no longer seemed to know what was happening. Her mind was filled with thoughts – none of them even remotely useful. She stumbled into the bedroom and found a pair of knickers to put on. She suddenly did not want to be naked. She had never felt more vulnerable than at that moment. She cursed her mother for getting her into this and then she cursed herself. She sat on the bed and cried because she could not think of anything else to do. Somehow, she eventually fell asleep.

It was early evening before Cassie awoke. She was not necessarily in a better mood but it was a stronger one. Amazingly, despite the emotional turmoil, she felt hungry. She also wanted a cigarette or two. She went into the kitchen and made herself an omelette – her favourite comfort food. Once that was devoured, she had a long warm shower. Outside, the sun was going down so Cassie put on the sexiest dress she had, a pair of lacy black French knickers and her red high heels. She then applied a thick coat of dolly bird makeup, some false eyelashes and tried to coax her hair into a reasonable shape. A quick look in the mirror confirmed that she was ready. She stepped purposefully out into the twilight.

"How are you this evening, Armand?" she called out as she passed her neighbour.

"I love the sound of high heels," he replied cheerfully.

Cassie turned more than a few heads as she sashayed her way towards the main square. It was amazing that men who had just spent the entire day in the midst of nudity could be so easily turned on by a woman in a flimsy frock and sexy shoes. She could hear the sound of some sort of show on the stage but that was not the sort of entertainment she was looking for. Instead, she went towards the restaurant and bar where there was a large outdoor seating area. It was there she saw Simone and her friends. After ordering a gin and tonic, Cassie strode over to their table where she was gazed upon with appreciation.

"You look ravishing," said Simone approvingly.

"This is how we dress on Saturday nights in swinging London," Cassie replied with some exaggeration. She was slightly disappointed to see that Simone was wearing much more casual attire – a pair of shorts and a tee-shirt emblazoned with some presumably suggestive French words.

"I think I need another drink," smiled Simone as she got up and moved towards the bar.

Cassie was glad of the opportunity to speak to Simone on her own and followed her. For her part, Simone recognised a layer of nervousness beneath Cassie's confident façade. Simone sipped her cognac and leaned lazily and slightly provocatively against the bar, waiting for Cassie to resume the conversation.

"Do you still sleep on a sofa?" Cassie asked, which was not the sort of question Simone was expecting.

"Yes," Simone replied with a slight frown.

"How would you like to sleep in a bed tonight?" Cassie whispered.

Simone's response was a broad smile. She finished her cognac and moved very close to Cassie. "I would like that very much," she purred, "if you were in the bed with me."

"Come on then," said Cassie, taking Simone's hand and leading her back to the bungalow.

In a little while, they were standing naked in Cassie's bedroom facing each other an arm's length apart. They had seen each other's bodies many times before but now they were looking at one another quite differently. Very slowly, they moved closer together until their breasts touched. Simone stroked the side of Cassie's face and then gently kissed her. A sudden shudder went through Cassie's entire body.

"Do not be afraid," Simone said soothingly. "It will be wonderful."

Simone led Cassie to the bed and an instant later they were lying entwined in each other's arms. Simone's kisses became more passionate and soon Cassie was responding with similar ardour. Simone knew exactly how to excite her. Cassie's previous experiences with women had been little more than teasing make-out sessions but this was the real thing. No man had ever made her feel this way.

Simone was right – it was wonderful. Cassie did not want it to stop but nothing can last forever, especially sex. The warm and sweaty afterglow was almost as good as the act itself. Cassie had to concede that John Fraser knew what he was talking about although this was probably not quite what he had in mind.

============================

CHAPTER EIGHT

Somewhere on the grounds of Le Soleil d'Or nudist colony in France, a dangerous enemy agent known only as the Fox was thought to be hiding. It was feared that he was planning some sort of sinister attack on a target as yet unknown. Fortunately, British Intelligence was working hard to identify the Fox and to stop his evil plans. Unfortunately, no one in London thought to inform the French authorities of the presence of British agents in their country. This, if it was discovered, could lead to a very awkward diplomatic situation.

Meanwhile, after her night with the passionate Simone, Cassie Pulaski had almost forgotten about the Fox and her reason for being in France. Things were not quite going to plan.

Some freshly baked croissants acquired on a quick dash to the resort's tiny bakery and a large bowl of rich French coffee had become Cassie's favourite breakfast. Simone was content with just coffee and cigarettes. At the age of thirty-two and single, her habits were well set. After breakfast, the two women shared a very soapy shower and Cassie once again marvelled at the sleek firmness of Simone's body. The French woman obviously did more than just play volleyball to keep fit.

After they had slowly dried each other off, Simone searched for her bits of clothing that had been abandoned so recklessly the night before and her expensive-looking watch. Cassie was surprised that Simone wore no other jewellery as most nudist women did. When Simone saw the time, she left out a loud and disappointed sigh.

The cats could not be bothered to rouse themselves from their slumber but Armand seemed as alert as ever. Cassie assumed that he was aware that she had an overnight guest but, despite her morning post-coital exuberance, she was not necessarily in the mood to talk about it. Instead, being English, she decided that the topic of conversation should be the weather.

"It's so beautiful here," she enthused. "I love this part of France. Usually when I've been here before, it was to go to somewhere by the sea. I love the sea and the beaches but it is so peaceful here and so, I don't know, refreshing."

"And you can be naked here as well," added Armand.

"That was not my primary reason for coming here," she replied, only slightly embarrassed.

"So why did you come to Le Soleil d'Or?" Armand gently pried.

"It's a long story," Cassie said defensively.

"I love long stories," smiled Armand mischievously. "People tell me their life stories all the time. They must think I'm some sort of priest or psychiatrist or perhaps they think that because I'm blind my mind does not work very well either."

"Oh, there's nothing wrong with your mind," said Cassie, lightly touching his shoulder and hoping to change the subject. "I'm sure there's much more to you than someone who simply sits and listens to the world go by."

"You're very perceptive," said Armand with a little laugh.

"I'm not as dumb as I look," replied Cassie, realising too late that comment did not come out right.

There was a brief pause as they smiled at one another. Then Armand's face took on a slightly more serious expression as though he was forming sentences in his mind before speaking.

"I was in the Resistance during the war," he finally said after a deep breath. "That is not as exciting as it may sound. There was not much action around here but it was a good way to meet women."

"Is that when you lost your sight?" Cassie asked cautiously, "during the war?"

"I was born blind," Armand replied almost wistfully. "I was a great disappointment to my father. He was a painter."

"An artist?"

"A house painter," laughed Armand, "like Hitler, although not as ambitious. My father had very modest goals but failed to achieve them. He died in the first war. My mother was so distraught that she felt unable to re-marry for almost a month."

Cassie felt she should be very careful with comments and questions during Armand's journey down memory lane. But her concept of tact was not necessarily the same as other people.

"Were you ever married?" she asked quietly.

"Only once," smiled Armand at the memory. "It did not last long. My wife could not understand me."

"Why not?"

"She was Chinese," replied Armand with that twinkle again. "She could not speak a word of French. But it was nice while it lasted."

Cassie began to doubt that she could believe anything that Armand told her. That did not lessen her enjoyment of the conversation.

"No wonder you live by yourself," she said in response to Armand's mischievous expression.

"I am not lonely," he shrugged. "I have my cats, pretty people stop to talk to me, and I enjoy sexual intercourse at least three times a week. I love nudists."

He reached out with uncanny accuracy and lightly stroked her bottom.

"Somehow," she said almost teasingly, "I don't think you will be adding me to your list of conquests."

"But, Chérie," he said without withdrawing his hand, "I have not yet completely turned on my charm. You have not even seen me dance my derrière."

"Your what?"

Cassie watched in amazement as Armand raised himself slightly in his chair and began to rhythmically bounce his bottom from side to side while he hummed some unrecognisable tune. It was a spectacle guaranteed to reduce any female to a fit of giggles.

"Not that old trick again," said a masculine voice from behind Cassie.

Armand laughed at the sound of the newcomer who came forward to embrace the old man. Although they were in a nudist resort, the stranger was fully clothed but did not seem to mind the others' nudity.

"This is my nephew Xavier," Armand said in Cassie's direction. "He is not really my nephew. We just say that so no one thinks we are queer."

"No one will ever suspect you of that, Armand," Cassie said warmly.

"I hope you will not think me queer either, mademoiselle," said Xavier in a cultured tone as he extended his hand to her.

Cassie shook his hand. It was not a firm grip. She had never known a man with such soft and well-manicured hands. He was a well-tanned chap, two or three years older than Cassie, with fairly classical features that he would never dream of hiding behind facial hair. He was dark blonde with hazel eyes and a seemingly permanent smile that could sometimes be interpreted as a smirk. Although he was obviously in a place for nudists, he was dressed in crisp and cool summer clothes that seemed to have been born in the pages of a stylish men's magazine. He had a low and soothing voice and Cassie immediately felt wary of him.

"My name is Cassie," she said politely.

"For real?" replied Xavier with raised eyebrows.

"Yes," Cassie affirmed, slightly offended.

"Cassie," he repeated quietly, "an unusual name for an unusual young lady.

For a moment, Cassie was afraid Xavier was going to kiss her hand but he merely let it go and went to stand on the other side of Armand, narrowly avoiding stepping on a cat's tail as he did so.

"What brings you to Le Soleil d'Or?" Cassie asked, suddenly reverting to spy mode.

"Xavier spends most of his life travelling," said Armand. "He often stays with me for a day or two when he is in this area."

"Do you travel for business or pleasure?" Cassie continued to prod.

"A bit of both," smiled Xavier, looking at her body with a curious detachment.

"And what exactly do you do?" Cassie asked, pushing her luck slightly.

"I am many things to many people," Xavier replied, as cryptic as he was annoying.

Xavier leaned forward and began to whisper to Armand in French. Unable to understand what was passing between them, Cassie decided that her presence there was superfluous.

"Well," she said, a trifle awkwardly, "I think I'll be going."

The two men smiled in her direction and then Xavier resumed his whispering. Cassie set off on her daily wander and wondered if the strange non-naked newcomer was worthy of a report to John Fraser.

Twenty minutes later, Cassie arrived at the recreation grounds. There was the usual buzz of naked activity on the various fields but no sign of Simone or her friends. Then Cassie caught sight of Biff standing by the low hedge that surrounded the mini-golf course. As usual, he was wearing a baseball cap but it was a different one.

"On your own?" Cassie said as she approached him.

Biff shrugged slightly. "Les is in one of his moods," he said with some irritation. "He thinks we should be moving on but I want to stay a little longer. I really like it here."

"You enjoy being naked?" Cassie asked playfully.

"I enjoy being naked around you," Biff replied, a smile finally forming on his frowning face.

His attention was drawn to a group of people playing mini-golf who were obviously having a wonderful time on the basic but cleverly laid out course.

"I really like miniature golf," he said ruefully. "I play it all the time back home. There are some crazy courses in Atlantic City – much more elaborate than this. This one is mostly about putting and angles but that can be fun too, I suppose."

"But it's no fun playing by yourself," Cassie surmised from the heavy hints.

"Not really," Biff replied hopefully.

"I've never played mini-golf," Cassie confessed. "You'll have to teach me."

"That's part of the fun," Biff said enthusiastically.

A couple of minutes later, Biff had acquired two putters and two brightly coloured golf balls – a red one for Cassie and a blue one for himself. He then led her to the small rubber matt that formed the tee for the first hole. He handed Cassie a putter and then stood behind her with his arms around her to help her to grip the putter correctly. Cassie did not require a great deal of instruction but Biff continued to prolong the lesson. Cassie was in a position to detect precisely how much he was enjoying the experience.

Once the lesson was over, they proceeded to play a round of what Cassie regarded as a sport more for children than adults. She may have formed that opinion because she was not very good at making the ball go where she wanted while Biff delighted in showing off his obvious skill. Still, Cassie preferred this naked game to volleyball and its leisurely pace allowed plenty of opportunity for chitchat and other verbal exchanges.

"So how did that project with the license plates turn out for you?" Biff asked as they studied the layout of the third hole.

"Unfortunately," Cassie replied as she hit her ball too hard and sent it over the boundary, "it was a bit of a non-starter."

"You know," Biff said, lowering his voice, "Lester thinks you're some sort of spy."

Cassie tried not to react to the comment. "What would a spy be doing in a nudist colony?" she asked in what she hoped sounded like an innocent tone.

"That's what we can't figure out," shrugged Biff.

For the rest of the game, Biff was content to merely flirt with Cassie. He was better at mini-golf than he was at flirting but Cassie was amused by his very obvious American manner. She was relieved that the course consisted of only nine holes rather than the customary eighteen. Even so, it was enough to give her a thirst for a very cold drink. They wandered over to the bar where she ordered two large lemonades with ice.

"I can't believe you can't get a Coke here," muttered Biff as they sat at a small table.

"That's all part of roughing it, I'm afraid," said Cassie as she lit a cigarette.

"At least the company is nice," smiled Biff.

Cassie smiled in return. If Biff only knew what she had been doing the night before, he might not be so eager.

"You're a woman of mystery, Cassie," he said as he looked her over. "You are nothing at all like the girls back home. You're so casual about being naked. I have trouble getting most chicks to take their bras off. Maybe that's my problem – going out with girls instead of women. It's not easy being twenty."

"Nothing is easy at any age," replied Cassie, sounding slightly like a fortune cookie.

"I think you're beautiful," Biff gushed. "I think you're my idea of a perfect woman – not only a great body but such a sexy accent. You've got fantastic legs and I just love the way your feet look in those shoes."

Please, dear God, thought Cassie to herself, not another boy with a foot fetish.

"You probably think I'm goofy," Biff said dejectedly.

"Not at all," smiled Cassie. "It's lovely to be appreciated and admired."

"You probably could have your choice of any man you wanted," he went on.

"Actually," Cassie said, almost to herself, "not so much."

Biff noisily drained his glass and rose to get another. He asked if she wanted a second lemonade but she politely declined and stood up to go. She had no desire to be on the scene when Biff suddenly needed to pee.

"I have to go," she shrugged.

"All right," Biff nodded, "I'll see you later."

"Yes," said Cassie, "maybe."

===========================

CHAPTER NINE

That evening, Cassie put on some perfume and a nice summer frock and made her way to the resort centre to indulge her never-ending appetite for ice cream. When she arrived at the café, she was disappointed to find that someone was sitting at her favourite table. Then she realised that it was Xavier – still wearing the same clothes as before – and decided to join him if only to try to gather a bit more information about this apparently shady character. Xavier seemed glad to have some company and watched in bemused wonderment at the amount of ice cream Cassie could consume in one sitting.

"I meant to say before," Cassie tentatively began the conversation, "that your English is excellent – hardly a trace of an accent."

"Thank you," Xavier replied with a toothy grin. "I speak several languages. I seem to have an ear for them and it helps in my work."

"What work is that?" Cassie asked, trying not to sound too curious."

"I am in the business of making life easier for other people," he said, still smiling.

"And how do you do that?" Cassie continued to pry.

"By doing anything I can," he shrugged, obviously wishing to change the subject. "Every client and every case is unique, you know?"

"No, sorry, I don't know," said Cassie, looking slightly less glamourous with chocolate sauce on her chin.

"Armand tells me that you are here by yourself," said Xavier, taking a sip of his vanilla frappé. "Do you often go on holidays on your own?"

"I'm between boyfriends at the moment," Cassie replied, staying close to the truth of someone who went through boyfriends the way other people go through a packet of cigarettes.

"Unlucky in love?" Xavier inquired.

"Not necessarily," said Cassie with a wicked grin. "I've had my moments."

"But have you ever been in love?" asked Xavier, clearly enjoying this topic much more.

Cassie looked up at the last traces on sunlight in the sky and took a deep breath. "I read somewhere," she said in a quiet plaintive voice, "that love is like the Loch Ness monster. It's a charming idea to believe in but it's never there when you go looking for it."

"You say that like someone who has looked often," replied Xavier without his usual smile.

"Once or twice," shrugged Cassie.

Xavier assumed what seemed to be a serious expression. "I've learned that you cannot make someone love you," he said quietly. "All you can do is stalk them and hope they panic and give in."

"Well," laughed Cassie, "that's better than most of the advice I've ever been given. You are either extremely wise or extremely crazy."

The smile returned to Xavier's face as he leaned back and lit a long thin cigar. "That is me, for sure," he said jauntily, "crazy like a fox."

Cassie suddenly felt a chill through her entire body. It could, she supposed, merely be a coincidence but the person she had come to regard as her best suspect had just uttered a very alarming word. Xavier did not seem to notice her reaction but he did mildly wonder why Cassie had suddenly lost her appetite for ice cream.

"How long will you be staying with Armand?" she asked, trying to disguise a slight tremble in her voice.

"A couple of days," he replied. "Three at the most."

"Then I might see you again," she said with a fake smile.

"I sincerely hope so," Xavier said in a tone that almost approached sincerity.

Cassie took the long way back to her bungalow both to allow her time to think and to avoid passing by Armand. Once inside, she slipped off her dress and shoes, lit yet another cigarette, and stared for a long time at nothing in particular. If anyone fit the profile of the Fox, it was Xavier but she had not the flimsiest shred of evidence, only a nagging sense of intuition. She would not sleep well that night but kept all the lights off so that she could sit by the window and watch Armand's bungalow. Surely the old man was not involved – he admitted that Xavier was a friend, not a relation. It would by typical of someone like the Fox to use a kindly old blind man as cover. The more Cassie thought about it, the more convinced she became. By the time Xavier returned to Armand's in the early hours, Cassie had decided to see John Fraser in the morning.

The man at the bicycle shop was slightly hesitant to rent another bike to Cassie but his reservation was removed by an additional ten francs. For the first time since she had arrived in Le Soleil d'Or, Cassie wore shorts. They were not just shorts but short shorts. The decision may have been prompted by Biff's comments about her legs or it might have been because it was easier to ride the bike with shorts. To complete the outfit, she wore a tie-dyed halter top and her sandals. Cassie may have been worried about the Fox but that was no reason not to look her best on this outing.

The journey to the village was pleasant if uneventful. All along the narrow road were very fragrant wildflowers in a variety of colours that were somewhat of a distraction. The slightly rolling countryside was not ideal for a novice cyclist but the chore of pedalling up one slope was rewarded with the pleasure of coasting down the other side. The only other person Cassie saw was a lorry driver standing beside his vehicle and relieving himself by the side of the road in the time-honoured French tradition. He actually waved as she pedalled past.

It took less time than she remembered to reach the village. As she approached the main street, she could see police cars and several gendarmes outside La Boule d'Or. They also saw her so she felt that turning around and leaving would only arouse suspicion. It never occurred to her to simply ride past and keep going.

She came to a halt on the edge of the outside seating area and saw Henri, the owner of the café who was looking more than a little distressed. A lone gendarme standing between them took one look at her legs and let her pass although her presence was noted by the gendarme's superior. Cassie quietly sat at the table with Henri. He looked at her with blurred vision as she reached across the table to pat his hairy hand.

"Henri," she whispered furtively, "why are the police here?"

"Your friend the Englishman is dead," Henri stammered in reply. "He has been murdered."

Cassie gasped loudly and tried not to do anything girlish or suspicious like fainting. Before Henri could tell her anything else, she became aware of someone standing beside her who was looking at her with intense interest. He said something to her in quick clipped French which she had no hope of understanding. Henri offered a rough translation.

"The Inspector wants to know who you are."

She looked up at him and decided that a smile was not appropriate.

"My name is Cassie Pulaski," she murmured.

"A Polish name," said the Inspector with some surprise, "and yet you speak to me in English."

"I am English," Cassie said, this time louder.

Henri and the Inspector conversed briefly in French, then Henri retired inside. The Inspector tried to offer Cassie a friendly smile but he lacked the personality for it. He settled himself into the chair next to her and stared at her in a way that would make anyone nervous.

"I am Inspector Lannes," he said as though he was expecting a round of applause, "and I would like to talk to you for a few minutes about this unhappy incident."

Cassie nodded in reply. Inspector Lannes was a short and swarthy greaseball impressed by his own importance. He liked to inform everyone that he was a direct descendant of one of Napoleon's marshals. He was single by choice although the choice was not his. He wore glasses, had an old-fashioned moustache, and walked with the aid of a stick.

"You know what has happened?" he asked curtly.

"Yes, I think so," Cassie replied carefully.

"How well did you know the deceased, this Michael Caine?" he asked, pausing only to check his notes.

"Who?"

The Inspector smiled stiffly. "I am prepared to accept that was not his real name," he sniffed. "I too go to the cinema. And I have already confirmed that he was not a part of Interpol as he apparently claimed."

"I knew him as John Fraser," Cassie said, hoping she was doing the right thing. "He never mentioned anything about Interpol to me."

"You were one of his lovers?" Lannes asked, giving her a long look that made her wish she had worn more clothes.

"I was just a friend," Cassie replied emphatically.

"Do you know his profession?" the Inspector continued, still referring to his notes.

"I believe he worked for a British company called Universal Exports," Cassie said, nervously counting how many gendarmes were on the scene.

"Truly?" Lannes snapped. "Then what was he doing here in the armpit of Languedoc?"

"I assumed he was on holiday," replied Cassie before she realised the stupidity of the answer.

"And you," the Inspector stormed, his voice becoming stronger, "are you on holiday as well?"

"Yes," replied Cassie with a whimper, "I am staying at Le Soleil d'Or."

"You are a naturist?" Lannes asked with some surprise.

"Yes," replied Cassie, almost defiantly.

"That, mademoiselle," he smirked as he sneaked a peek at her legs, "is the first thing you have said that I believe."

There was a lengthy pause while Lannes made a series of entries in his well-used notebook. He was obviously not a local policeman but had been brought in because someone somewhere decided this was not just any murder but a case that required experienced handling. Lannes may have been an odious individual but he clearly knew his job and Cassie could tell from the demeanour of the gendarmes that they respected him. His notes complete, the Inspector returned his attention to Cassie.

"The murder weapon was a knife," he said in a suddenly soft tone. "The killer was very proficient – I think there was possibly some sort of torture involved. It will take poor Henri a long time to get rid of all the blood."

Cassie suddenly felt sick but she tried hard to control herself. She did not think the Inspector considered her a suspect but he clearly realised she was not being totally honest with him. He carefully regarded her every reaction as he mentally tried to assemble all the pieces of a puzzle that, once put together, would still fail to make any sense. He knew this was no ordinary murder and that there was something going on that he would possibly never understand.

"You are returning to England soon?" he asked, hinting that the interview was nearly completed.

"Yes," Cassie nodded repeatedly, "soon."

"The sooner the better," Lannes said gently, "for you and for us."

He rose from the table and escorted Cassie to her bike which a gendarme was helpfully holding upright for her. She was about to leave when Lannes suddenly spoke again, as if something had just occurred to him.

"Are you a religious person?" he asked.

"Not really," replied Cassie, uncertain where that line of questioning came from. "I attended a Catholic girls' school but we didn't have enough nuns to go around. I was mostly taught by left wing anarchists – or nihilists – one or the other."

"I'm an agnostic," the Inspector said wistfully, "but I sometimes find prayer to be very soothing."

He abruptly turned away from her and returned to the crime scene. Cassie pedalled quickly until she was outside the village then she stopped by the side of the road for a little cry and vomit. She did not know what else to do and wondered when or if London would be informed about Fraser's death. She had no way of contacting them – she was well and truly on her own. Her minimal training had not covered this contingency. All that she was certain of was that the Fox was somewhere nearby and he might or might not know all about her.

==============================

CHAPTER TEN

Cassie arrived back at Le Soleil d'Or in time for lunch. She thought she had been gone much longer. Despite the shock she had endured, or perhaps because of it, time had dragged by like a lazy and malevolent sloth. Food had a very limited appeal at that moment – unlike drink. Cassie opened a bottle of wine, nearly filled the largest glass in the bungalow, then loudly cursed when she discovered that there were only two cigarettes left in her last packet. The only good thing about the day so far was that she did not see John Fraser's lifeless body.

It was inevitable that Cassie's thoughts should turn to escape. She wished she had gone with the four hippies in their Volkswagen bus. She considered joining Biff and Lester on their hitch hiking tour of Europe. If only she could somehow reach a city with a British consulate, she might be safe - unless, of course, the Fox was already watching her. That seemed, for the moment at least, unlikely. If the Fox knew who she was, she would probably be dead like poor John Fraser.

She wondered about Xavier who was not very far away from her. Was he too obvious a suspect or merely someone who stood out in a crowd – a fully dressed person in a nudist colony. Would the Fox draw attention to himself that way? She was wary of him but strangely not overly afraid of him. But she had to wonder what was underneath his clothes.

The problem was that even if Cassie knew for certain who the Fox was, there was virtually nothing she could do about it. She had no weapons and her only link to British Intelligence had been terminated. Discovering the identity of the Fox was not a secret worth dying for.

"Cassie," she said to herself as she undressed in front of the mirror, "what the bloody hell are you doing here?"

Her thoughts were interrupted by a knock on the door. As Cassie debated the wisdom of answering it, there was another not quite as polite knock which soon became fairly insistent. Unable to bear the noise, Cassie threw the door open and found a somewhat bedraggled Biff standing there with his backpack.

"Hey," he said limply.

"Biff," she said, surprised, "you're not leaving, are you?"

"Actually," Biff mumbled in a sleep-deprived tone, "I was kind of hoping I could move in here – temporarily."

"Why?" asked Cassie, genuinely concerned, "What has happened?"

"My good friend and bosom buddy Les has somehow managed to get himself a girlfriend," he said with real irritation. "Three people in a tent is definitely a crowd, especially when two of them are constantly screwing."

"You better come in," Cassie said like a mother hen. "I'll make us some coffee."

Biff dumped his backpack just inside the door and all but collapsed on the sofa. He gratefully accepted a mug of strong coffee even though he would have preferred a beer. Cassie sat next to him and lit a cigarette from the packet she had discreetly lifted from Biff even though she had left another one burning itself out in the kitchen.

"Who is this girl?" she asked gently.

"I don't know," shrugged Biff. "I think maybe she's Jewish like Les. She's small, dark and pointy."

Cassie decided not to investigate that description any further.

"She was in one of the other tents at the campsite," Biff continued, "with this weird guy Ivan."

"Ivan?"

"Yeah, you know," he replied with mild disgust, "that blonde brooding guy with the guitar. She said she broke up with him because he never listened to her. At least, I think that's what she said."

"What's her name?" an intrigued Cassie asked.

"That's funny, I'm not sure," Biff shrugged, squinting his eyes in concentration. "She probably told me her name but it is just possible I was distracted by her tits."

"So you don't like her but you like her breasts," Cassie commented.

"She's all right, I guess," Biff conceded reluctantly. "To tell the truth, I wouldn't mind banging her myself which I should have done because I saw her first. But the stupid bitch seems to prefer Les for some reason."

"I can't think why," Cassie said in her best comforting tone.

"They never stop talking," Biff went on with annoyance, "except when they're screwing. They talk about politics – some really serious stuff. I think she may be a commie. She sure as hell doesn't have many morals. Les is in absolute pussy heaven, pardon my French."

"Are you jealous?" Cassie asked quietly.

"Me – are you kidding?" he almost exploded. "Are you suggesting the Biffmeister is jealous? You bet your sweet bippy I'm jealous. I'm fucking jealous!"

"Is that why you've come to me?" Cassie asked in a friendly but non-committal manner.

"You're the only other friend I've got here," Biff sighed. "I mean, I guess I could have moved in with Ivan but that would be just sad and weird."

"We must talk about Ivan later," Cassie said. "How well do you know him?"

"How well can you know a guy who almost never talks?" he replied with a quizzical look.

Biff continued to sip his coffee while Cassie stretched out her legs and took a deep breath. She was grateful for the distraction and even more grateful for the company. She really did not want to be alone at that point in time and she actually found herself warming to Biff despite his habit of staring at her the way men do when they are mentally undressing a woman. After all, she was already naked. But it was her face that Biff was mostly looking at.

"I hope you don't mind me saying this," he said in a halting voice, "but you don't look so hot."

"I've had some bad news," Cassie replied in a tone that implied she did not wish to pursue the topic.

"Sorry to hear that," Biff said politely.

Cassie went into the kitchen and tried to make herself busy by tidying up the very few things that required tidying. Her various thoughts were confusing her now but she was beginning to regard Biff's arrival as a stroke of luck and, at the moment, she needed all the luck she could get. The fact that she was half American and Biff was all American also seemed to be an advantage. At least they both spoke the same language – sort of.

She came back into the living room and resumed her seat next to Biff who had hardly moved since arriving.

"I don't mind your staying here," she said quietly. "In fact, I would be glad of the company. My only worry is that it might be slightly dangerous for you."

"No shit," replied Biff, only slightly alarmed, "in what way dangerous?"

"I think someone may be trying to kill me," Cassie said as simply and unemotionally as she could.

Biff burst out laughing. "Why would anybody want to do that?" he asked in between guffaws. "I mean I can dig somebody wanting to get into your pants – figuratively speaking – but killing you seems a tad extreme."

"Well," shrugged Cassie, "you've been warned."

Cassie got up again while Biff's laughter gradually died down. He was suddenly concerned that he had offended her and crossed the room to stand behind her with his hands gently resting on her shoulders.

"Sorry about that," he said weakly. "I guess I thought you were kidding."

"It's all right, Biff," she replied.

"I guess I'll be sleeping on the sofa, huh?" he asked.

"I guess," nodded Cassie.

Biff moved an inch or two closer which allowed him to look down at Cassie's body from a very interesting viewpoint. It was almost as good as teaching her to play mini-golf but he had something quite different in mind.

"Would you like me to paint your toenails?" he asked breathlessly.

They both seemed surprised when Cassie agreed but she had always found it extremely difficult to resist any form of pampering. Cassie gathered up her favourite red nail polish and they went out onto the patio where the light was much more conducive to artistic endeavours. Cassie settled in her chair while Biff knelt like a happily debauched servant in front of her. He was very good and very meticulous in his work which he clearly did not regard as a chore. Cassie was almost enjoying the experience but she could not decide which worried her more – the slightly crazed look in Biff's eyes or his fully erect penis.

Biff was just putting the finishing touches on Cassie's little toe when they were joined on the patio by Xavier who was, as usual, fully dressed. Biff looked up at him with even more suspicion than Cassie.

"Bonjour," he said cheerfully, regarding the painting activity with interest.

"Hello," replied Cassie, her body tensing slightly.

"I have no wish to disturb you," Xavier said in his overly pleasant voice, "but I was in the office a little while ago and Jean-Luc asked me to deliver this to you."

He took a small envelope from his pocket and handed it to Cassie. She immediately recognised it but pretended it was nothing important.

"Merci," she said quietly.

"It is my pleasure," smiled Xavier with a slight bow. He then made his way to Armand's bungalow and went inside.

"Who's that guy?" Biff asked.

"That's a good question," Cassie replied.

Biff remained kneeling for a moment to admire his handiwork then stood up so that Cassie could see the result of his efforts – efforts which he seemed to enjoy far too much.

"You may have found your calling, Biff," Cassie said admiringly.

"It's just a hobby," shrugged Biff with a shy smile.

Biff went inside for an alleged pee which gave Cassie an opportunity to open the envelope. It contained a small card with a typewritten message: "The church in the village, tomorrow at noon – Uncle Silas."

Cassie let go a sigh of relief. British Intelligence had made contact with her. They obviously knew about John Fraser and had new instructions for her, possibly even an exit plan. Her mood was immediately much better. Not only was the end possibly in sight for her secret mission but she had the prettiest toes in all of Le Soleil d'Or.

After a couple of minutes, Biff came back onto the patio. He also looked somewhat relieved. He leaned against the wooden railing and looked out at a world full of nature and nudity.

"So," he said with some enthusiasm, "what are we going to do now?"

"Well," replied Cassie, still admiring her bright and gleaming toenails, "if you are going to be staying with me, we should probably go down to the market and stock up on supplies."

"Sounds good to me," said Biff, extending a hand to help Cassie out of her chair. "We can pick up some beer and potato chips."

The quite different tastes of Cassie and Biff became apparent during their grocery shopping expedition as each tossed items into their basket that made the other frown or grimace. Cassie was uncertain how long Biff had intended to stay with her as he seemed to be stocking up for a long siege. When they reached the till, Cassie was more than happy to accept Biff's offer to pay for everything. Her main concern was how to carry it all back to the bungalow.

As they struggled with their bags on leaving the market, they encountered Simone and her two friends who were on their way in. Simone lingered to smile suggestively at Cassie and to look with mild disbelief at Biff.

"Where have you been, Chérie?" she asked pointedly. "I have missed seeing you."

"I've been busy," replied Cassie, nearly collapsing under the weight of her bags.

"So I see," purred Simone with another long look up and down at Biff. "I hope I shall find you again soon in more pleasant circumstances."

As Simone disappeared inside the market, Biff moved closer to whisper in Cassie's ear.

"You better watch yourself with that chick," he said as if confiding a secret. "I've heard she's a lezzie."

"Yes," replied Cassie quietly, "I've heard that too."

"I'll never understand lesbians," Biff went on as they made their way back to the bungalow, "but I bet they're a hell of a lot of fun to watch."

"You're a very silly boy," laughed Cassie.

============================

CHAPTER ELEVEN

As predicted, Biff spent the night curled up on a sofa that was more comfortable for sitting than for sleeping. So he did not mind too much being awakened earlier than usual by Cassie slamming the door on her way out to purchase fresh croissants after having first turned on the fairly noisy coffee maker. It was still, he decided, better than sleeping in a tent with Lester, especially when Lester was passionately involved in a salacious relationship.

Biff had never had croissants until a few days earlier and he had fallen in love with them. They were pastries worth waking up for. Cassie had wisely returned with half a dozen of them knowing that Biff would easily devour three. He ate on the sofa while Cassie took her breakfast out onto the patio. It was a slightly overcast morning but the air was still warm and the French sun – unlike the uncooperative English one – would soon burn through the clouds to produce a lovely day.

Her houseguest indulged in a much longer shower than she did and he also did things in the tiny bathroom that she would prefer not to know about. Cassie had briefly lived with men in the past and none of them impressed her with their morning habits. At the same time, Biff found Cassie's makeup and hair rituals to be highly amusing but he was somewhat confused to see her putting on knickers and her most demure summer frock.

"Going somewhere?" he asked.

"I have to go to the village," Cassie explained as though addressing a child.

"Are you going to hitch hike?" Biff wondered aloud.

"Don't be silly," scoffed Cassie lightly. "I'm going to hire a bike like I always do."

"Cool," said Biff, his face lighting up. "Can I come too?"

Cassie debated the wisdom of Biff accompanying her. On the one hand, it was probably a breach of the rules but on the other he might provide a modicum of protection. Not only that, he had the delightful habit of making her laugh.

"All right," she said with a smile. "Put some clothes on. You do have some fairly nice clothes, don't you?"

"I've got a tee-shirt I haven't worn yet," he beamed as he searched through the rumpled contents of his backpack. "I was saving it for a special occasion."

At the bicycle shop, Cassie was given her usual bike. Biff had been hoping for a ten speed racing bike but had to settle for an old-fashioned bicycle with touring handlebars and coaster brakes. They rode the bikes out of the resort and onto the road at a medium speed with Cassie in the lead.

There was little chance for conversation as they rolled along the nearly deserted road towards the village. From half a mile away they could see the tower of the church although Biff had no idea that was their destination. He was literally along for the ride and enjoying both the splendours of the countryside and spending time with Cassie.

She signalled for them to stop slightly short of the main street where they both drank from their water bottles while Cassie assessed the situation. The village seemed quiet enough as they walked their bikes towards the church. The centuries old structure was crumbling in places but it was still the most impressive building in the village. Unfortunately, the clock in the tower no longer possessed any hands but the tower itself was a monument to survival. It was the sort of church to which the ecclesiastical authorities sent problem priests or those on the verge of retirement.

They approached the church carefully. A tall thin severe looking woman who bore a passing resemblance to a praying mantis was waiting on the steps. Cassie and Biff rested their bikes against a stone wall then Biff followed Cassie towards the woman.

"Who is this?" the woman snapped, scowling at Biff.

"A friend," replied Cassie.

"You were told to come alone," the woman said peevishly.

"Actually, I wasn't" Cassie pointed out correctly.

The woman stared directly and coldly into Biff's eyes. "Go away," she ordered.

Biff looked to Cassie who nodded slightly. He slowly slinked away in the direction of La Boule d'Or, taking his bike with him. Once he was a safe distance away, the woman turned back to Cassie.

"For the purpose of this meeting," she said in a cold monotone, "you may address me as Vanessa. That is, of course, not my name."

She looked like a City solicitor from a firm that dealt with corporate rather than criminal law. She wore a smart suit, sensible shoes, and had her hair pulled back tightly away from her decidedly plain face. Her only concession to being in a warm climate was wearing a large pair of very dark sunglasses. She carried a standard department-issue briefcase that had seen better days as had the Ford Cortina with British number plates that was parked nearby. She looked Cassie over carefully and sighed with disappointment.

"We know all about Fraser," Vanessa said coolly. "That was a most unfortunate turn of events. But the department feels your mission can still be successful."

"Not if I get killed too," Cassie protested weakly.

"We are hoping it will not come to that," replied Vanessa who did not like being interrupted. "I am going to give you some materials that may help you – Fraser's notebooks, recent relevant reports from some of our European operatives, and – against the advice of several people including myself – a gun."

She partially opened the briefcase so that Cassie could see the neatly assembled files and the matt black Beretta.

"The gun is not loaded," continued Vanessa as if delivering a lecture. "The ammunition is in the case in an unmarked box. If you find that you must use your gun, try to keep track of how many rounds you fire for the accounting department."

"Thanks a bunch," mumbled Cassie to herself.

Vanessa handed her the briefcase along with another of those little envelopes.

"This is probably the most important thing," she said, lowering her voice. "It's the direct telephone number to ring once you have identified the Fox. Your need not eliminate him – just identify him so that we can track him or her."

"I've got one fairly good suspect," Cassie said, hoping to add something positive to the meeting.

"I trust you are not referring to Xavier Villon," Vanessa snapped back. "We know all about him. He's harmless. Very attractive, but harmless – relatively."

There was a long and awkward silence. Vanessa was obviously impatient and seemed to have little confidence in Cassie who, in turn, had developed an instant dislike for Vanessa, which saved time.

"Do you have any questions?" Vanessa asked after looking at her watch for the third time.

"Just one," replied Cassie in a calm voice. "Are you going to be my new contact here?"

Something resembling a smile crossed Vanessa's face for the first time. "No chance," she smirked. "You're all on your own, ducky."

"Thanks a bunch."

Vanessa turned abruptly and went to her car. It did not start immediately and Cassie quietly prayed it would break down or, even better, blow up. But it did start eventually and Vanessa sped out of the village driving, as many English people in France do, on the wrong side of the road.

Cassie got her bike and slowly pedalled to the café, steering with one hand and holding the briefcase with the other. She joined Biff who, having seen her coming, had ordered a large cold drink for her. He had watched the hush-hush meeting from afar and was amazed by what he saw.

"You really are some sort of spy," he said, overflowing with admiration.

"I suppose I am in a way," Cassie sighed. "I don't feel much like one though."

Henri, the café owner, delivered Cassie's drink and offered a sympathetic smile.

"How are you, mademoiselle?" he asked.

"I'm all right," Cassie replied with a wry smile of her own, "but I've been better."

"I have just the thing for you," Henri beamed with pride, "a magnificent lunch that I have prepared myself – for you and your friend – on the house, as you say."

"Merci beaucoup, Henri," smiled Cassie.

Henri practically danced back inside to his beloved kitchen. Cassie took a long drink and felt her body finally beginning to relax.

"I wonder what we're getting," said Biff with a worried expression.

"I have no idea," sighed Cassie, "but whatever it is, you will eat every bit of it and enjoy it – or else!"

"Yes, ma'am," nodded Biff with a grin.

The lunch was magnificent as so many French lunches are. Cassie could not pronounce the names of any of the delicacies set before her but that did not diminish her enjoyment of them. Biff was less enthusiastic but pleasantly surprised by some of it. The wine was also very good which was probably why Cassie gave Henri such a big kiss and hug before they left. She did not even mind Henri clutching her bottom.

"Sacred blue," Biff said, mostly to himself, "what the hell does that mean anyway?"

The wine also affected their return journey. They walked much of the way and the progress was slow but they arrived at Le Soleil d'Or without incident or accident.

When they returned to the bungalow, Cassie went directly into the bedroom and closed the door. She then proceeded to undress and to empty the contents of the briefcase onto the bed. For the next several hours, she pored over the papers and files and came to the inevitable conclusion that no one knew anything more about the Fox than she did.

She finally left the bedroom, made a brief visit to the bathroom, then went into the living room. Biff was sitting on the floor with his head against the sofa as if he were watching television even though the bungalow did not have one. Cassie sat next to him but neither looked at the other directly. Biff had just lit a cigarette which Cassie casually took from him. She took a long drag and exhaled a cloud of smoke that hung over the two of them like a threat.

"Are you ready to tell me what's going on?" Biff asked.

"It's a long story," shrugged Cassie.

"You're a spy," said Biff in a friendly rather than an accusing way.

"Well," smiled Cassie, "maybe not so long."

"I want to know everything," Biff said quietly. "I think I deserve that."

Cassie nodded. She then proceeded to relate the whole saga from her meeting with Sir Alistair to her encounter with Vanessa including her various suspicions and the death of John Fraser. The only detail she chose to omit was her night of passion with Simone. Biff listened silently with the wide-eyed wonder of a boy seeing a movie for the first time. For her part, Cassie was surprised that her long story did not take as long to tell as she had anticipated but she was relieved to finally be able to tell it to someone. When she was finished, she waited for a reaction from Biff. When none was immediately forthcoming, she got up to pour a glass of wine for her very dry throat.

Biff came into the kitchen and stood behind her which seemed to be a favourite position of his. But instead of merely placing his hands on her shoulders or giving her a friendly hug, he reached around and cupped her little breasts in his hands as he leaned forward to kiss her throat like a very romantic vampire. Once again, it was very obvious how much she had turned him on – it is a secret that is difficult for nudists to keep.

Cassie did not resist Biff's attentions – if anything, she welcomed them. But it was simple human contact she craved more than sex. If sex was the only way to procure that, she was more than willing to participate. She turned to face him and they kissed properly and passionately with their bodies pressed hard against each other. No words were exchanged but they both knew the bedroom would be a better setting for this scene. Cassie cleared all the papers and the briefcase off the bed with a few sweeps of her arms. Biff picked up the pistol, looked at it for a moment then tossed it aside in favour of something much more exciting. Cassie was lying on the bed and he rushed to join her.

Biff was an enthusiastic if somewhat clumsy lover with a seemingly limited knowledge of foreplay. His treatment of her nipples was especially painful. Cassie consoled herself with the thought that the act itself would not last very long. But once Biff was inside her, he seemed to be there forever. Cassie had assumed she would need to fake an orgasm but that turned out to be unnecessary. In his limited experience, Biff had never encountered a woman who was as vocal in bed as Cassie.

They both longed for a cigarette afterwards but the packet was in the other room. Biff volunteered to fetch it and returned carrying a can of beer as well. At least, Cassie thought to herself, he was not one of those blokes who simply rolled over and went to sleep. But he also did not seem to understand a woman's need to be cuddled. That was something Cassie never asked for – she demanded it. Biff put his beer down to wrap his arms around her as they both smoked and stared at the cheaply framed print of a landscape that hung slightly askew on the wall that faced them.

Biff quickly lost interest in the painting and returned his attention to Cassie's body that was stretched out beside him. There was nothing about it that he did not like.

"Tell me something," he said, almost in a whisper, "about that woman at the church."

"What about her?" asked Cassie, slightly bristling at the memory.

"Did she even notice your toenails?"

Cassie looked at Biff for a moment and then began to laugh. For a little while at least, she was no longer worried or afraid. Things could only get better from now on. She might even seduce Biff into an encore performance in celebration of her much improved mood. Suddenly she seemed able to put the search for the Fox into some sort of perspective. Finding him was not the most important thing in her life unless, of course, she ended up dead as a result.

She threw herself onto Biff's body and forgot about everything else.

===========================

CHAPTER TWELVE

"I really love James Bond movies," Biff said in between bites of his morning croissant. "Is what you do anything like James Bond?"

"Not even remotely," replied a grateful Cassie.

"So what's our next move, boss?" Biff asked with a wide crumb-encrusted grin.

It was a question Cassie had asked herself repeatedly. There was no obvious answer and she was not certain she should include Biff in any plans she might make. But, she realised, it would be difficult to exclude him at this point after the two of them had become so friendly.

"I think," she said slowly, making it up as she went along, "it might be an idea to check out this Ivan bloke. He's our best suspect at the moment."

"Okay," nodded Biff approvingly. "We can check on Les while we're there and maybe pump that chick of his for information."

"Pump?" asked Cassie.

"It's an expression," shrugged Biff innocently. "After all, she was with Ivan before she was with Lester."

"Right," said Cassie, trying to sound positive, "that's what we'll do then."

Even on a secret mission, Cassie was not going out without first seeing to her makeup and hair. Biff was glad to see that she had decided to wear her red shoes on their little expedition. He pulled on his white tennis shoes than spent two minutes deciding which of his baseball caps to wear.

Cassie and Biff were an odd couple as they emerged into the sunlight of what Cassie had come to refer to as another bloody beautiful day. She kept intending to buy a pair of sunglasses at the resort shop – after all, what is a spy without sunglasses? – but she always seemed to forget when she was actually there. They walked past Armand's bungalow and she noticed that neither the old man nor Xavier was on the patio although the cats were, lazily devouring their breakfast.

The campsite was not quite as crowded as before, probably because it was mid-week and many campers were only there on weekends. Two rather attractive but very pale teenaged girls were lying in the sun next to a large tent and Cassie was mildly annoyed at the attention Biff was paying them. They found Lester sitting cross-legged in front of his tent looking none too happy.

"What's happening, man?" Biff asked in a jock and jocular sort of way.

"Not much," replied Lester glumly.

"Where's the filly?" asked Biff as he sat beside him while Cassie chose to remain standing.

"You mean Reba?" Lester said with a grimace. "She's gone."

"What happened?" Biff's voice was suddenly full of concern. "I thought the two of you were tight."

"We were," nodded Lester. "It was good for a while, really good. Hell, it was great. I never knew how much fun a girl could be."

"So what went wrong?" Cassie asked.

Lester looked up at her with embarrassment. "We had a sort of...philosophical disagreement," he said.

"What about, man?" laughed Biff, doing absolutely nothing to improve Lester's mood, "about politics?"

"No," replied Lester sheepishly, "oral sex."

Cassie covered her mouth with her hand to keep from laughing but Biff was more sympathetic, putting a friendly arm over Lester's shoulder.

"I told you about that stuff, didn't I?" Biff said like a knowledgeable big brother. "You have to please chicks if you want them to please you. Man, it's like a mortal sin to say no to a girl, especially Jewish girls. Hell, you should know that better than anybody."

Lester said nothing but simply hung his head dejectedly. While Biff tried to comfort his friend with the old "more fish in the sea" line that no one ever believed, Cassie wandered a few steps away to survey the campsite.

"He's gone," she said to no one in particular. "Ivan's gone."

"They left as soon as the sun came up," Lester said.

"They?" asked Cassie.

"Yeah," replied Lester with a scowl. "Reba went back to him last night. Then this morning, off they went in his Skoda."

"What's a Skoda?"

"It's a Czechoslovakian car," Cassie answered like a school teacher. "God help them if they break down." She crouched down in front of Lester and took his hand in hers. "Do you have any idea where they went?"

"I think they're headed to the Riviera," Lester replied sullenly. "Apparently, that's a good place for swingers."

"Swingers?"

"Yeah," scoffed Lester. "It turns out that Reba and Ivan were married. Ain't that a kick in the head?"

Cassie got up and moved away from the two boys to think. Once again, her best lead had turned into a dead end. Or was it? Ivan could still be a prime suspect but, if he was, he had slipped through Cassie's delicate little fingers. She then realised that she probably had the license plate number of Ivan's Skoda on the list they had made. She could telephone that information to London and they could track him, just in case. It was not much but it was something.

Meanwhile, Biff and Lester were still in best buddy mode.

"What do you think you're going to do?" Biff asked.

"I don't know," shrugged Lester slightly petulantly. "It's obvious you're in no hurry to leave. I thought about hitching back to Paris or somewhere and getting a plane home."

"You can't do that, man," Biff said in his most positive voice. "This is a happening place. It's better even than California."

"Yeah," replied Lester, glancing over at Cassie, "you're doing okay."

"I told you, man," enthused Biff, "fish, sea, lots." He motioned towards the sunbathing teenagers.

"I don't know, Biff," sighed Lester. "I think Reba is going to be a hard act to follow."

"But it was good while it lasted, right?" said Biff with a manly nudge.

"Yeah," Lester replied with a slight smile, "it was fucking great while it lasted. It just didn't last very long. It never does."

Cassie came back to stand next to them. The two boys looked up at her with not very different thoughts in their not quite mature minds.

"I have to make a phone call," Cassie said in a very business-like tone. "I'll have to use the call box outside the office. You can either stay here or meet me there."

"I'll meet you there, babe," Biff replied with a familiarity he hoped would impress Lester.

Cassie set off as quickly as she could in high heels on unpaved ground. The boys watched until she was out of sight because, as far as they were concerned, she was the best sight around. Biff smiled to himself as he decided on a new topic of conversation with his morose friend.

"Hey, Les," he said slyly, "do you remember when you said that you thought Cassie was some kind of spy?"

"Yeah."

"Well," Biff continued in a low voice, "it turns out that you were right."

After dashing back to the bungalow to retrieve a scrap of hopefully vital information and then hurrying to the public phone near the main square, Cassie's call was received with minimal interest by a seemingly mindless duty officer who never even thanked her. A bit of etiquette in the espionage trade would not go amiss, thought Cassie, as she decided her labours deserved to be rewarded with ice cream. She was halfway through her sundae when she was joined by Biff and Lester.

"I told Les all about it," Biff announced with a boyish grin.

Cassie was not pleased that her secret was not quite so secret anymore but she realised it was the only plausible explanation for her sudden relationship with Biff. The two boys had been somewhat helpful before and, with John Fraser no longer on the scene, they were the only help she was likely to get.

"Do you have a code name?" asked Lester whose mood had improved remarkably.

"Yes," nodded Cassie, "sitting duck."

Cassie glanced over towards the recreation ground and saw Simone and several friends playing badminton, a spectacle that would have warmed the hearts of Biff and Lester if they had looked in that direction. In her mind, Cassie thought that Simone would be the ideal person to help her but revealing her secret to her would probably have been an unforgivable breach of security.

It was quite possible that Simone also saw Cassie. If she did, she would continue to wonder why her lover of one fantastic night now seemed to prefer the company of a pair of callow youths – and American youths at that – even though the one with glasses did appear to be exceptionally well endowed. Simone and her red-haired friend were dominant in their doubles match against a pair of fairly sturdy Dutch girls.

There were many other people to look at besides a quartet of lesbians hitting a birdie over a high net. Le Soleil d'Or was filled with potentially interesting people and it was still possible that the elusive Fox was one of them. Being naked, Cassie concluded, was probably the best disguise the Fox ever had.

Perhaps the Fox was not so naked. Despite what the disagreeable Vanessa had said, Cassie could not entirely dismiss her suspicions about Xavier. For that matter, she was not certain how much she could trust Vanessa. In her new job, Cassie was discovering that it was virtually impossible to trust anybody with the possible exceptions of Biff and Lester, who were too young and far too naïve to be spies, and Henri the owner of La Boule d'Or who made magnificent lunches. She had previously been reluctant to confront Xavier on her own but now she had Biff and Lester to back her up and, if necessary, she had a gun.

"Let's go," she said abruptly.

They found Xavier and Armand together on Armand's patio. The old man was sitting in his usual chair but Xavier was standing with a suitcase beside him. The suspicious trio approached them full of false smiles and friendly but insincere nods.

"Going somewhere?" Cassie asked nonchalantly.

"Alas, yes," smiled Xavier. "Duty calls."

"I have an unopened bottle of that wine you like so much," Cassie said like a professional tease. "Perhaps you would like to come over for a farewell drink."

"I would enjoy that very much," replied Xavier with his usual grace, "if my good friend Armand does not mind too much."

"Why should I mind?" Armand said with half a growl. "I'm an old man. I've had enough wine to last a lifetime. Besides, it would only make me want to piss and I've already had my half hour's piss for the day."

"Well then," said Cassie, holding out her hand.

Cassie led Xavier to her bungalow with Biff and Lester following close behind. Once inside, she suddenly and quite roughly shoved Xavier into a chair and, with her two companions, proceeded to surround him. He made a couple of attempts to rise only to be pushed back into the chair by Biff who was possibly enjoying the experience too much.

"Would you mind telling me what is going on?" asked Xavier with very obvious anger.

"You tell us," Cassie replied coldly, "just who the hell you are exactly and what you're doing here."

"You are not serious," laughed Xavier.

"We're deadly serious, buddy," said Biff with the menace of a schoolyard bully, "or should I say Monsieur Fox?"

Xavier's laughter only increased to the point that he had tears in his eyes. He looked at the three of them and shook his head as he tried desperately to regain his composure.

"Sacré bleu," he finally gasped. "God save us from the Americans. And you, my dear Cassie, I thought you would know better or, at least, know something."

"What do you mean?" Cassie asked, suddenly confused.

"I thought British Intelligence trained their agents better than this," Xavier replied in a calm voice, "or that at least they taught you some subtlety."

"You know who I am?" stammered Cassie. "I mean, what I am?"

"Of course, my poor little kitten," smiled Xavier. "I have always known. I am here for the same reason. I am from the Directorate – the French secret service."

"Can you prove that?" asked Lester sensibly.

"Can you prove I am not?" smiled Xavier. "We have been hunting the Fox even longer than you. We received the same intelligence as you that the Fox was likely to be here in Le Soleil d'Or. So I was sent to investigate."

"And what did you find?" Cassie asked quietly.

"I could find nothing," shrugged Xavier with another of his annoying smiles. "If the Fox was here, he is long gone. But I seriously doubt that he was ever here. In fact, I sometimes wonder if the Fox actually exists or is merely a creation of our enemies made with the intention of having us chasing our own tails."

"Or," said Biff who refused to let go of an idea that appealed to him, "you could be the Fox telling us a bunch of lies."

"My dear young friend," Xavier scoffed, narrowing his eyes, "if I was the Fox, you would not be keeping me in this chair so easily. You would all be dead like that poor English fellow in La Boule d'Or."

Cassie continued to stare at Xavier. She wanted to believe him if only because what he said made sense and because Vanessa seemed to know all about him. She did not like making mistakes but she disliked looking foolish even more. She motioned for Biff and Lester to step back which allowed Xavier to get up and to smooth out his clothes.

"I believe you said something about some wine," he said as if nothing unpleasant had happened.

"Sorry," shrugged Cassie, "I lied about the wine."

"In that case, Chérie," he smiled, "I will be on my way. As I said before, duty calls."

He moved towards the door, slightly brushing past Biff and Lester as he did so. He opened the door and then made a little bow towards the others with a mild flourish.

"Au revoir, mes amis," he said with another laugh.

"Can I ask you something," Cassie said suddenly. "Why, when you are in a nudist resort, do you always insist on wearing clothes?"

"I will tell you the truth only because I am leaving and none of us will ever see each other again," Xavier said, his smile fading. "I wear clothes in a nudist colony for the very simple reason that I am a proud man who had the misfortune to be cursed with a very small penis."

Before anyone could say anything, he was gone. The others shuffled about awkwardly.

"Well," Biff said after a lengthy pause, "that sucked."

"I wonder if he's right," mused Cassie quietly, "that the Fox has either gone or was never here in the first place."

"Or never existed," added Lester.

"If that were true," Cassie said as she turned over several thoughts in her head, "then who killed John Fraser or, more to the point, why kill him at all?"

"It's a mystery, all right," sighed Biff.

"Yes," nodded Cassie with annoyance, "and if there is anything I hate, it's bloody mysteries."

===============================

CHAPTER THIRTEEN

Cassie had offered to let Lester sleep on the sofa in her bungalow but he preferred to return to his tent saying that the scenery was better at the campsite. Biff was relieved to hear it. However, the sleeping arrangements were the least of Cassie's concerns and, despite Biff's frequent and somewhat lewd remarks, sex was also very far down her list of priorities. There were only two things she wanted to do: identify the Fox and return to London. She would have been more than happy to merely accomplish the latter.

"Actually," Cassie said as Lester prepared to go, "I think it might be best if you went back to the tent too, Biff."

"But I thought..." Biff began to protest.

"I want to be alone," replied Cassie like Greta Garbo.

"Whatever you say," Biff mumbled.

As soon as the boys were gone, Cassie began to miss them. She had no idea why she dismissed them. She had acted on impulse and acting impulsively was a habit she had been trying to break for years because it invariably led to trouble. She was left alone with just her thoughts and her cigarettes, neither of which provided much comfort. Even her shoes suddenly felt uncomfortable so she kicked them off, leaving her completely naked in more ways than one. She was the one thing she never ever wanted to be again – she was vulnerable.

I must be made of sterner stuff, Cassie thought to herself. I am the daughter of two successful international spies. Surely some of that shit must have rubbed off on me.

Cassie wished she had paid more attention when her boyfriends took her to see those James Bond movies. She stared out the window and saw Armand sitting alone on his patio. A slight bit of inspiration struck her as she walked out the door without bothering to put anything on her feet and quickly went over to him.

"Bonjour, Armand," she said gaily.

She leaned over to kiss his wrinkled cheek which gave the old boy the opportunity to gently stroke her tight little bottom. As he did so, he delighted in breathing in her perfume.

"Have you come to make love to me?" he asked hopefully.

"Not today," Cassie replied as she gave him back his hand. "I just want to talk."

"Ah, well," Armand sighed, "conversation is a form of intercourse. We take what we can get."

Cassie shooed one of the cats off the only other available chair and pulled it up close to Armand. She wanted to reach out and hold his hand but both of his hands were in his lap and she was afraid of grabbing the wrong bit of him.

"You said you were in the Resistance during the war," she began slowly. "Was it very dangerous?"

Armand smiled wryly at his memories. "If it had been easy," he said, "everyone would have done it. We lived in constant fear of being caught. Some of us were luckier than others."

"So how did you survive?" she asked, deeply interested. "What was the secret of being undercover and not being found out?"

"The secret was to behave perfectly normal," Armand sagely replied, "to do nothing to attract attention – to never, even for a moment, to do anything that might be regarded as suspicious. When we were in public, even if there were no Germans or collaborators about, everything we did had to appear normal. We never knew who was watching. I was luckier than most. After all, who would suspect a blind man?"

Cassie detected more than a hint of pride in Armand's voice and manner. He was relating things as though they had happened yesterday. His last comment in particular seemed to unnerve her. She sat back in her chair and looked at him intently.

"Armand," she said quietly, "are you the Fox?"

"The Fox?" he frowned. "What are you talking about?"

"You are, aren't you?" Cassie gasped as though she had seen the light on the road to Damascus.

Armand laughed slightly. "My name is Armand Ferrand," he said in a calm and even tone. "I am a blind old nudist with a weakness for cats and young women. As much as it pains me to say it, that is all I am and all I am ever likely to be."

Cassie took a deep breath as she tried to release the tension from her body. Her momentary and rash jump to the wrong conclusion had worried her but it had also briefly excited her. For one split second she had thought that she had accomplished her mission only to end up feeling foolish at how completely wrong she had been. How could Armand possibly have been the Fox? How could Cassie possibly have been so stupid to even think it? So much for her intuition. Trying to unmask the wrong people was becoming a habit.

Armand shifted slightly in his chair as one of the cats jumped into his lap.

"Now that I think about it," he said quietly, "Xavier talked about a fox when he was here. He's involved in espionage, you know."

"Yes, I know," Cassie replied sullenly.

"The trouble is," smiled Armand, "he's not very good at it. I'm surprised he has not been killed or transferred to a desk job."

Cassie's mind started to work again. "You said he's not your nephew," she said carefully. "Is he your son by any chance?"

"I have often wondered that," Armand replied wistfully. "He is the son of a woman in our Resistance group. She was very generous with her favours – she slept with all of us. She used sex to forget about the war. She was very forgetful. Sadly, she did not survive. Those of us who did took turns looking after Xavier. Any one of us could be his father."

"That's very sad," Cassie said.

Once again, the two of them lapsed into silence. The only sounds were the birds in the trees and the loud purring of the fat ginger cat in Armand's lap.

"Are you a spy too, ma petite?" he finally asked.

"I'm more of a trainee," Cassie shrugged.

"Are you sure you would not like to make love?" Armand said with a smile. "It will not take very long and you are making me very randy."

"I have to be going," Cassie replied as she got out of her chair and looked down at him.

"Eh, bien," sighed Armand in resignation. "I am here if you want me. But please, dear Cassie, be very careful."

"That's my plan," she said with a little laugh, "practically my only plan."

It was not until Cassie had returned to her bungalow that she realised she was still barefoot. Her feet were dirty and her painted toenails had begun to lose their lustre. She put on a pair of sandals and then went wandering aimlessly around the grounds of Le Soleil d'Or. She was looking at all the people differently now. The one thing that stood out from her conversation with Armand was that truly suspicious people seldom looked suspicious.

There were new faces and familiar faces but all of them belonged to people who were merely nudists whether they had the bodies for it or not. Cassie began to think that she had been wrong to listen to her superiors and to confine her search to Le Soleil d'Or. Perhaps the Fox was simply nearby in a convenient hiding place like a villa off the beaten track. It was a thought worth pursuing.

Cassie went to the bicycle shop. The owner had now taken to smiling at her and wheeled out her usual bike as if presenting it to royalty. For some reason, she thanked him with a Spanish *gracias* – foreign languages always confused her – and proceeded to walk the bike slowly back to her bungalow. She may have become accustomed to being a nudist but she was still very far from wanting to ride a bike in the altogether.

She dashed quickly into the bungalow to put on a halter top and a pair of white Capri pants that, until that moment, she had forgotten she had packed. She sighed as she realised she had once again forgotten to buy sunglasses.

At the main road, she turned left instead of right as she usually did to go to the village. She wanted to explore a bit of the countryside she had not seen before – a fairly sparsely populated part of the countryside with open fields alternating with thick wooded areas. There were a number of dirt roads leading off from the main road. Most of them lead to quaint little houses with charming gardens. A few simply had dead ends with an occasional ruin and one followed a small stream whose water was clear and cool as it gurgled along.

It was frustrating to discover that nearly everyone who had a house in that part of Languedoc lived in the middle of nowhere. Every house appeared to be a perfect hideout for someone up to no good or merely the home of people who valued peace and quiet. It would take an army of agents to investigate them all and that would hardly be a discreet operation unlikely to endear them to the local authorities.

After nearly two hours of finding nothing more than countless lovely places to live, Cassie returned to Le Soleil d'Or. She stopped at her bungalow only long enough to undress then went to return the bike to its rightful owner. She decided she had earned herself a large ice cream and went to her favourite café for a large sundae swimming in Belgian chocolate sauce and whipped cream with not one but two cherries on top. All that was missing was a little paper umbrella.

She was accomplishing as much by gobbling up the frozen goodness as she had on her cycling tour of the immediate vicinity. For the first time during her stay at Le Soleil d'Or, she idly wondered if all the ice cream she was consuming was in any way affecting her weight. She looked down at her body and saw no difference or, at least, nothing worth worrying about.

She was halfway through her sundae and suffering a mild case of brain freeze when she saw Jean-Luc out of the corner of her eye. He was carrying another of those little envelopes. Cassie had no idea how they arrived at Le Soleil d'Or – that was another mystery of the secret service. Jean-Luc dropped the envelope on her table, gave her a vaguely disapproving look, and waddled off. Cassie looked around carefully before slitting open the envelope with a long and sharp fingernail.

The message was: "You will be extracted in forty-eight hours. After that, the mission is redundant. Uncle Silas."

Cassie could not decide whether to be disappointed or happy. On the one hand, she was going home – back, as it were, to civilisation. On the other, it seemed to indicate that her mission had been a failure or, perhaps, there was new information on the whereabouts of the Fox which indicated that a continued presence at Le Soleil d'Or was a waste of time. The whole thing, Cassie concluded, had been a complete waste of time, money and energy – not to mention the loss of John Fraser. But at least she was coming out of it with a fabulous all-over tan.

She thought about telling Biff and Lester the good news but decided that could wait. She was too full of ice cream. Instead, she fancied a pleasant nap before dinner. She walked slowly and carefully back to her bungalow, trying not to belch or fart because either of those would be most unladylike. She was only partially successful.

As she entered the bungalow, Cassie became aware of a sharp and sudden pain on the back of her head. She pivoted and fell onto the hard wooden floor.

==============================

CHAPTER FOURTEEN

Cassie almost did not recognise Simone with clothes on. The French woman was wearing a stylish and flattering dark pants suit and a pair of elegant black low-heeled shoes. Her makeup and hair were impeccable. She was also brandishing a large and deadly looking knife with a serrated edge. Meanwhile, Cassie was still naked, aware of a splitting headache, and tied unnecessarily tightly to a chair.

They were in a room that was obviously nowhere in Le Soleil d'Or. It was sparsely furnished and a heavy curtain effectively blocked out the light from the only window. Cassie correctly guessed that she was in one of the houses she had seen on her cycling tour earlier that day. She neither saw nor heard anyone else and assumed that she was alone with Simone who was pacing about slightly and looking at her with cold dark eyes and a slight frown.

"You disappoint me, Cassie," she finally said.

"I'm not exactly thrilled with you either," Cassie replied with forced bravery. "I never thought you would be the Fox."

"I never cared for that nickname," Simone scoffed.

"I can think of other things to call you," Cassie said, trying to put some substance into her trembling and weakened voice.

"You should be careful how you talk to me, Chérie," snapped Simone, flashing the knife. "Your little life is in my hands. I will decide whether you lose it slowly or quickly."

Cassie decided to obey the old adage about saying nothing if you could not say anything nice. Simone's expression became less stern as she continued to pace about the room, fondling the knife like a favourite dildo and glancing occasionally at her uncomfortable captive.

"I suspected there might be a British agent nearby," she said calmly. "I never thought it was you."

"What gave me away?" Cassie asked with genuine interest.

"Nothing you did," Simone replied in an offhand manner. "You were informed on."

"You tortured John Fraser into telling you," Cassie said accusingly.

"I admit I tried," shrugged Simone, "but he was loyal to you until the end. No, my information came from London."

"London?" gasped Cassie.

"You remember my good friend Sonia, the girl with the red hair," Simone went on, clearly enjoying herself. "She frequently went to London and other places to meet some of her contacts. I think perhaps you know her London contact – an oily little man with a bald head."

"The man in Sir Alistair's office," said Cassie with sudden realisation. "He's a mole?"

"Nothing so complicated," smiled Simone. "He is merely one of those men who likes to trade secret information for – what do you call them – blow jobs. Such a stupid and inaccurate expression."

"So what happens now?" Cassie asked, not really wanting to know the answer.

Simone looked at her expensive watch thoughtfully. "In a few hours," she said in a calm voice, "I shall be far from here doing something important but you will still be here. You understand that what I must do to you is nothing personal. It's my job."

"You didn't have to bring me here," Cassie protested weakly. "You could have just slipped away and I would never have known who you really are. I was being recalled to London anyway."

"Yes, I know," nodded Simone. "But you are a loose end, my dear Cassie, and I do not like loose ends, especially ones I have been to bed with. When the police eventually come here, they will find Sonia in another room."

"You're insane," Cassie hissed.

"That is not a very nice thing to say," Simone retorted with the slightest hint of anger, "especially to someone with whom you have been so intimate."

"I faked my orgasms," Cassie said spitefully. "I faked the whole thing."

"I do not think that is true, my darling," purred Simone like an almost tamed tigress. "But if it was, it is another reason to slit your lovely throat. You should thank whatever god you pray to that I am not Jacqueline the Ripper."

Simone gripped the knife more tightly and moved closer to Cassie, almost close enough to strike and certainly close enough to see the fear in her wide brown eyes. Cassie lowered her chin in an attempt to reduce the target as her hands struggled in vain to free themselves. Cassie's only thought was to somehow delay the inevitable.

"Before you kill me," she gasped between her short breaths, "aren't you going to tell me what you were planning? In the James Bond movies, the villain always brags about his fiendish plot."

"I am sorry you see me as a villain," replied Simone, "after all we have been through."

"I'm sorry you're going to cut my throat," sobbed Cassie.

"The plan is actually a simple one, as all the best plans usually are," said Simone proudly. "I am going to..."

Simone never finished that sentence. She was interrupted by the soft popping sound of a pistol with a silencer. A 9mm round entered her forehead and terminated her brain activity. Her fall to the floor was not graceful.

Cassie squirmed to look behind her and saw a woman holding a smoking gun. She was good looking, in her late forties with old-fashioned hair and minimal makeup. She wore a plain dark grey dress that looked almost like a uniform. Cassie recognised her immediately.

"Mum!" Cassie cried out.

Annie Pulaski rushed to free Cassie from the chair. The two women then had a tearful reunion and a prolonged and very firm embrace.

"Where have you come from?" Cassie struggled to ask.

"I have been here for some time," Annie replied quietly. "I heard about this mission of yours so I decided to keep an eye on you. I was always very effective in the shadows."

"They told me you were missing," Cassie said with confusion, "that nobody knew what happened to you."

"Sir Alistair has always known what happened to me," Annie scoffed. "I fell in love with someone from the other side, so I defected. I've been living in Minsk for the past five years. It is hard to imagine a more dreary place than Minsk. I felt that if I wore any colour other than dark grey that I would stand out from the crowd."

"Do you ever think about coming back?" Cassie asked hopefully.

"Not really," Annie shrugged. "Minsk is marginally better than prison. Besides, I'm still in love – with someone else. Not only that, I would hate to throw away all that time and effort I put into learning Russian. It's a difficult language. And that alphabet...!"

They smiled at one another and it was only then that Cassie began to feel embarrassed about being naked. Her mother sensed this and casually went over to Simone's body and removed her jacket which she then placed gently around Cassie's shoulders. They shared another hug then wandered outside to breathe in some fresh air and to momentarily forget about death. The sun was low in the sky and the clouds were painted with a variety of colours.

Cassie looked at her mother and frowned. "Won't those people in Minsk or wherever be, well, annoyed that you killed one of their agents – one of your agents?"

"Simone was shot with John Fraser's gun," Annie explained calmly. "They will think the British did it. The important thing was that I had to protect my daughter."

"I've missed you, Mum," said Cassie, almost in tears.

"Oh, darling," replied Annie with emotion, "I've missed you too. You are my only regret in all of this. You have turned into a fine young woman, if a trifle promiscuous."

"Mum," scoffed Cassie playfully, "it's the Sixties. Haven't you ever heard of free love?"

"I've heard of it," smiled Annie. "I just could never afford it."

As they talked, they strolled down the dirt track leading to the main road. When they were out of sight of the house, they came upon a battered old Citroen. Annie approached it and opened the door on the driver's side.

"Come on," she said in a perky voice, "I'll give you a lift back to your bungalow."

It was just a short drive back to Le Soleil d'Or and Cassie was surprised that she could think of so little to say during the journey. She would have imagined having a million questions for her mother but only one kept coming to mind.

"Will I ever see you again?"

"I wish I knew the answer to that, sweetheart," Annie replied with a sigh. "It's a crazy world. Who can predict the future?"

"You're not staying, are you," Cassie said solemnly.

"I've stayed too long already," Annie said in a similar tone, "but it was worth it."

A couple of minutes later, Annie brought the car to a halt in front of Cassie's bungalow. They sat there for a long time, staring straight ahead in silence.

"You're not coming in?" Cassie finally asked.

Annie shook her head. "You better give me Simone's jacket so I can return it to the scene of the crime. Then I have to get back to Minsk as fast as this old wreck can take me."

Cassie slipped off the jacket and handed it to her mother. They shared a final embrace then Cassie tearfully struggled to open the door of the car. Annie pulled her back in for one more kiss.

"When you see Sir Alistair," Annie said on the verge of breaking down, "give him my love and tell him I'll always treasure the memory of Istanbul."

Cassie was in no mood to take messages. She threw her arms around Annie as though she never intended to let go of her.

"I love you, Mum," she said tearfully.

"And I love you, monkey chops," replied Annie.

A few minutes later, Cassie was standing on her patio watching the battered old Citroen disappearing along the wooded track. Then she went inside and cried for a very long time, pausing only to drink wine and light cigarettes. Even when the tears subsided, she found it impossible to sleep. She had been inches away from death and she had found her long-lost mother only to lose her again. It was a day that would be imprinted on her memory forever.

Cassie decided that she really did not like being a spy. As the long sleepless night wore on, she began to understand the appeal of mind altering drugs. The only problem was she did not have any.

============================

CHAPTER FIFTEEN

The next day was Cassie's last day at Le Soleil d'Or. She felt a little bit like Dorothy on the verge of leaving Oz. Early that morning, she was one of the first to buy a couple of fresh croissants from the bakery. They and two cups of strong black coffee seemed to revive her spirits as did a long hot shower. It was another day and she was very glad to be there to see it. But now most of her thoughts revolved around going home.

Cassie took a long look at her naked self in the mirror and was pleased with what she saw. Then she put on her red shoes and set off on the now familiar route through Le Soleil d'Or. Everything suddenly seemed different. She seemed different. For perhaps the first time, she was actually enjoying being there.

She felt comfortable being naked among naked people and she was at last able to look at them without wondering if any of them was worthy of suspicion. They were just people on holiday with no clothes on. Some of them, she had to admit, would do the world a favour by putting some clothes back on. It was a bit of a paradox that some of the most enthusiastic nudists were the ones who should not be doing it at all. But nudism was nothing if not the epitome of tolerance. "Let it all hang out" was a popular maxim of the day and the people at Le Soleil d'Or were certainly doing that.

Even Jean-Luc looked good that morning as he approached her carrying a larger than usual envelope which he roughly thrust at her without a single word of greeting.

"Thank you," Cassie said politely.

"I hope this is the last one," he replied gruffly. "I am not a postman, you know. I have other things to do."

With that, he scurried back into his office like a vampire anxious to avoid the sun. Cassie went a little farther along the path until she came to a small wooden bench in the shade of an overgrown plane tree. She carefully opened the envelope to find a railway ticket from Béziers to Paris and an aeroplane ticket from Orly Airport in Paris to London Gatwick but no note from Uncle Silas. The tickets were for that afternoon. She would need to ask Jean-Luc one final favour – to arrange for a taxi to take her to Béziers.

She was surprised when she entered the office to find Jean-Luc deep in conversation with a fully clothed Inspector Lannes. The two men both rose as she came in and Lannes was not subtle in the way he surveyed Cassie's naked body for the first time. As Jean-Luc busied himself on the telephone to the local taxi company, Lannes moved closer to Cassie.

"So you are leaving," he said like a true detective.

"Yes," replied Cassie breezily. "I'm going back to London today."

"I am relieved to hear it," sniffed Lannes. "Your presence here is having an adverse effect on the local homicide rate. There have been two more murders nearby."

"Really?" said Cassie. "That's shocking."

Cassie did her best to pretend she was surprised by the news but she was never very good at deception, something of which Lannes was all too aware. His bloodshot eyes narrowed as he stared at her.

"My inclination was to detain you," he said in his most officious manner, "but my superiors told me not to. The case is now being handled by very secretive officials from Paris."

Cassie said nothing and was relieved that Jean-Luc's phone call ended at that moment.

"Your taxi will be at your bungalow at one o'clock," he said. "I wish you bon voyage."

"Merci, Jean-Luc," Cassie replied sweetly as she turned to go.

"I also must be on my way," said Lannes who waved slightly to Jean-Luc before escorting Cassie out into the bright sunshine. He paused to look at all the naked people doing their various naked activities and sighed heavily.

"I do not understand nudists, mademoiselle," he said with a shake of his head. "I do not understand them at all. Perhaps you can explain them to me."

"What makes you think I'm a nudist?" laughed Cassie.

She quickly moved away from him, carefully clutching her envelope, and continued on her way through the resort. When she entered the campsite, she saw Biff and Lester sharing a large blanket in the sun with two blossoming French teenaged girls who had become attracted to the boys when they found out they were Americans. Lester was concentrating on a game of chess with one of the girls while Biff was busily painting the toenails of the other. When he saw Cassie standing by their tent, he quickly got up and went over to her, a move that did not please his new friend.

"I've come to say goodbye," Cassie said simply. "I'm going back to London."

"What about your mission?" Biff asked with surprise.

"It's over," shrugged Cassie, almost embarrassed by the admission. "I found out who the Fox was. It was Simone. She's dead."

"Wow," said Biff, raising his eyebrows, "I guess it's a bad idea to mess with you."

"I just wanted to thank you," Cassie continued in a soft uneven voice, "for being there."

"I didn't do much," Biff replied awkwardly. "Not as much as I wanted to."

There was an uneasy moment of silence before Cassie pulled him closer and gave him a big sloppy kiss which did not go unnoticed by the girl with the half-painted toenails on the blanket. Biff moved to embrace Cassie but she stepped back away from him.

"You better get back to your friends," she said quietly.

"Yeah," nodded Biff. "Have a safe trip and, well, thanks for the memories."

Cassie smiled brightly and left. She strolled rather than walked back to her bungalow along the path that would take her past Armand's. As she arrived, he was giving a goodbye, morning after kiss to a deliciously overripe woman of about forty who was looking very pleased with herself. She smiled at Cassie as she went past and then Armand's face lit up as he sensed the approach of Cassie's distinctive perfume.

"I've come to bid you adieu," she said brightly.

"I am very sorry to hear that," sighed Armand.

"All good things come to an end," smiled Cassie.

"And you," Armand grinned widely in return, "are certainly a very good thing."

"I'm going to miss you, you silly old rascal," she said teasingly.

"And I, ma petite, will always regret that you and I never made the beautiful love together," replied Armand very wistfully.

"Would it please you, Armand," she whispered as she moved in to kiss his cheek, "if I told you I was tempted?"

"You women will be the death of me," he laughed. "There are worse ways to go."

"Adieu, mon ami," Cassie said in between two final kisses.

By one o'clock, Cassie was packed, dressed and waiting for her taxi which was only ten minutes late. As the car left Le Soleil d'Or, Cassie resisted the urge to look back. She had a long journey ahead of her and her only regret was forgetting to bring a trashy novel to read on the way.

She arrived safely at Gatwick Airport and marched through the terminal wearing her favourite red high heels. She was met by a solemn looking man in a grey suit who escorted her to a car driven by a nearly identical grey-suited man. The drive to London passed without a single word of conversation. Cassie was almost relieved to arrive at the building where she had worked for several years. The two men gallantly allowed Cassie to carry her suitcase as they walked with her to Sir Alistair's office.

The boss greeted her with a faint smile and motioned for her to sit as the two grey suits discreetly withdrew.

"You did very well for a female," Sir Alistair intoned. "Very resourceful. It is a pity about Fraser. Damned bad luck."

"I quit," Cassie suddenly said. It was a quiet voice but she thought she was shouting.

"I beg your pardon?" Sir Alistair gasped.

"I quit," Cassie repeated as she stood up and left the room, slamming the door behind her.

Cassie used the last of the money from her mission to pay for a comfortable black taxi to take her home. She returned to her modest one bedroom flat in Ilford. It somehow seemed much nicer than before. She stood in the middle of her compact sitting room and breathed a massive sigh of relief. Then she proceeded to slowly remove all her clothing.

===============================

THE END

===============================

<u>ALSO AVAILABLE:</u>

Printed in Great Britain
by Amazon

43131997R00076